Wines

by

HENRI FLUCHÈRE

Illustrated by the author

Under the general editorship of

VERA R. WEBSTER

This title originally published
in the Golden Guide series.

GOLDEN PRESS • NEW YORK
Western Publishing Company, Inc.
Racine, Wisconsin

FOREWORD

I have tasted nearly all the wines described in this book at one time or another. Some are, alas, either geographically or economically beyond my reach. For these I have based my reporting on the opinion of friends and experts whose wine sense and discriminating palates I trust completely.

Since, in the final analysis, a wine is evaluated subjectively, I have tried to refrain from making statements reflecting my very personal likes and dislikes, leaving the ultimate judgement of any wine to you, dear reader and fellow-adventurer into the delightful world of wine. *A votre santé!*

H.F.

 Produced in the U.S.A. Published by Golden Press, New York, N.Y.

Library of Congress Catalog Card Number: 72-85934.

CONTENTS

INTRODUCTION

In the fortunate regions of the world where favorable conditions for grape cultivation exist, generations of men and women have enjoyed wine, without fuss or posturing, as part of their daily meals. In the countries of these regions wine is considered a food.

Most of the wine produced throughout the world is a good, plain, and relatively inexpensive beverage, much like the plain food it usually accompanies so agreeably. Fancy, premium wines are rarer, somewhat more expensive, and truly great wines are rarest, and most expensive, drunk on special occasions by those who can afford it.

The world's wine regions are located, with few exceptions, within the narrow climate bands shown in the map below, where the average annual temperature is between 50° and 68° Fahrenheit.

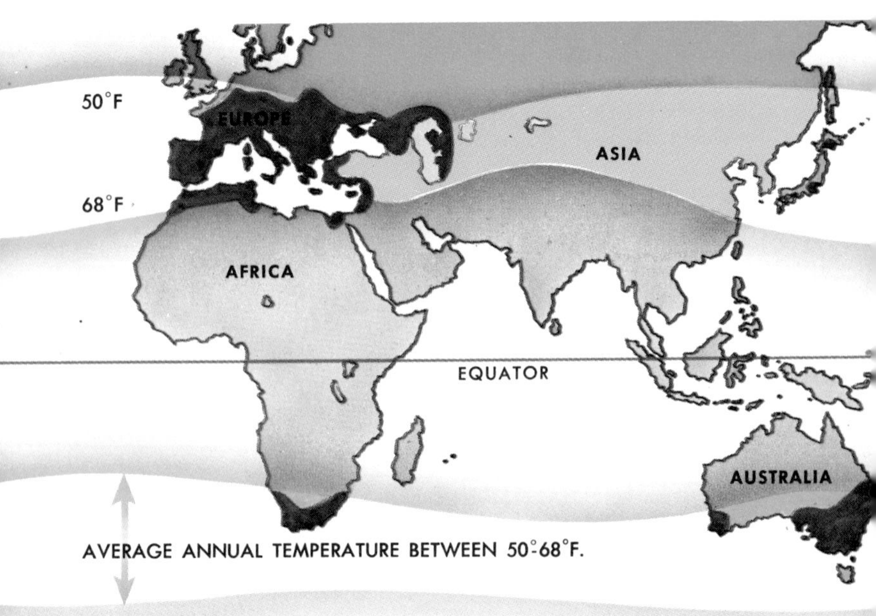

Taste preferences differ from one region to another, and from individual to individual, in wine as well as food. Nature, aided by man, has met this challenge with a profusion of grape varieties. Climate, soil, and other variables cause further differences in the taste characteristics of the wine produced by any given grape, providing an almost infinite range of taste sensations.

Some wines are big and robust, like Italy's *Barolo*; some are light and delicate, like the *Chenin Blanc* of California; some are sweet, and some are austerely dry. In between these extremes lies a whole range of delightful taste gradations, providing a choice for every palate's satisfaction and preference, and blending with the varieties of the world's foods.

A few regions successfully manage to grow wine grapes beyond the ideal climate bands in each continent because of special weather conditions, or by planting resistant varieties of vines.

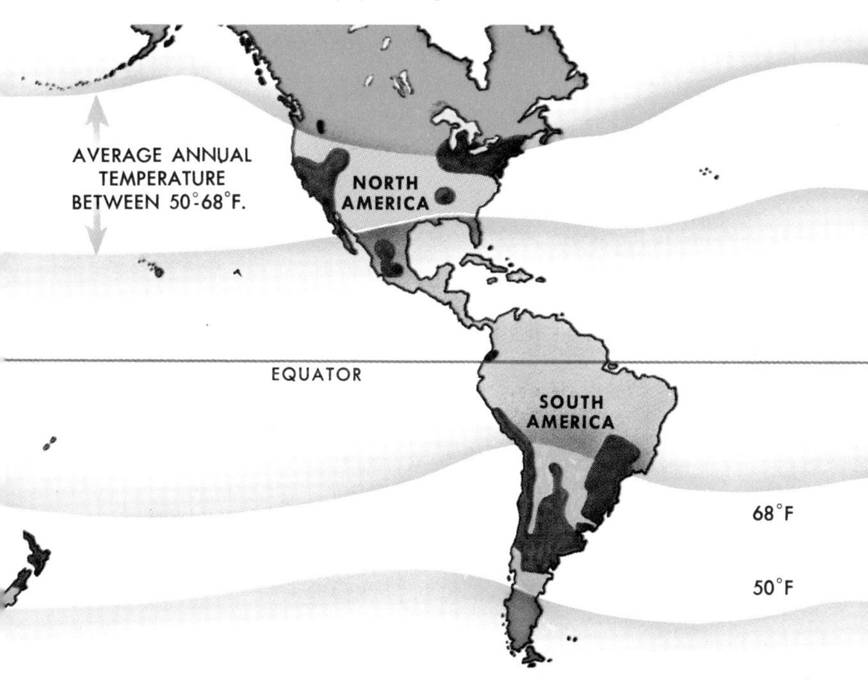

Wine Making

The evidence of man's discovery of wine lies still buried in some dark antediluvian strata, but archeologists have unearthed fossilized grapes leaves, seeds, and other fragments showing that a grape vine, closely resembling today's species, awaited man's coming. We can surmise that the great discovery was made shortly after man learned to make containers that would hold liquids safely.

Historically there is ample evidence of the ancient cultures' appreciation of wine. The Egyptians depicted scenes of viticulture and wine making in friezes dating back to circa 2,500 BC. The Bible is replete with references to wine, wine making, and wine drinking.

THE GREEKS of Homer's time had mastered the art of making non-porous pottery which enabled them to age their wines and ship them to distant places such as Egypt which had by then lost the art of wine making.

THE ROMANS were quick to learn from the Greeks, and under the *Pax Romana* vineyards flourished from Italy to England. Pliny, the Roman naturalist, described 91 grape varieties and over 50 wines.

THE GAULS were beer drinkers but soon learned to prefer wine. Good coopers, they used their barrels when they switched from brewing to wine making. The gallic wines became so famous that, in a fit of parochial pique, the emperor Domitian decreed that their vines were to be uprooted. The Gauls revolted, and since no occupying Roman really wanted to enforce the decree, the vines continued to flourish.

IN THE DARK AGES, following the fall of Rome, the monastic orders established the great traditions of wine making still upheld to this day. Many of the finest vineyards were started by the monks, particularly the Carthusians, and have continued to produce some of the world's finest wines.

THE GRAPE

"Good wine begins with good grapes," is a vintner's maxim backed up by the fact that a wine of superior quality has yet to be made from inferior grapes. There are thousands of grape varieties but the limited number of high quality grapes cultivated for the finest wines are all derived from the genetic stock of the old-world species, *Vitis vinifera,* except for some outstanding varieties of *Vitis labrusca* in North America.

The hybrids are mostly man-made varieties, created as a countermeasure to the dread *Phylloxera,* a burrowing plant louse which all but wiped out *vinifera* vineyards all over the world in the late 1800's. The *labrusca* species are resistant to this plague. Almost all high-quality grapes grown today, in any of the world's wine regions, are grafts of *V. vinifera* on disease-resistant root stock, or hybrids. Agricultural research stations are improving and developing disease-resistant stock.

MAJOR VARIETIES of grapes, both pure stocks and hybrids, are shown here and on the pages following, with a listing of some of the wines made from them. Only a few can be shown, or listed, because of space limitations, and their order has no bearing on their relative quality, importance, or popularity.

Note that some grapes produce both red and white wines, and sometimes rosés as well. Some produce generic wines, some varietals, and some both. There is a strong trend in wine making today toward increased production of high-quality varietals, particularly in California and the Eastern United States.

PINOT CHARDONNAY. One of the great white wine grapes. In France it produces the famed Chablis, Pouilly-Fuissé, Corton-Charlemagne, Montrachet and other great white Burgundies, as well as Champagne. In New York and California it is usually labeled as a varietal, and some goes into the finest U.S. champagnes. Like most of the fine varieties, it has a small yield, making the wine expensive.

PINOT NOIR. This is the grape of the great red Burgundies, the Romanée-Conti, Corton, Chambertin, Pommard, Nuits-Saint-Georges, etc., the excellent California varietals and the finest California Burgundies. It also produces top quality rosés and whites, and a major portion of French Champagnes. This low-yield grape is planted in the Loire Valley, Alsace, Germany, and many scattered locations throughout the world.

CABERNET SAUVIGNON. The best and most widespread of the Cabernet variety, responsible for the finest Médocs and the best clarets of California, Australia, and many other regions of the world. **CABERNET FRANC** *(not shown)*, a close relative, makes a softer wine. It is not yet planted in the U.S. but enjoys a slowly growing popularity in the Médoc, Graves, St. Emilion, and Pomerol regions, and in the Chinon reds and rosés of the Loire.

RIESLING grapes produce the most distinctive white wines of the Rheingau, Moselle, and Alsace. It is a widely grown variety in such different climates as Australia, Austria, Chile, California, New York and Switzerland. The name often appears on the label, and in California where the **SYLVANER** variety can, for some obscure reason, be legally called Riesling, the name given the true variety is **JOHANNISBERG RIESLING** to differentiate it from imitations.

SAUVIGNON, also called Sauvignon Blanc, a superb white wine grape, is the major ingredient of the best Graves, and a constituent of Sauternes with Sémillon and Muscadelle. It yields the Loire's Pouilly-Fumé, Sancerre, and Quincy. In California's North Coastal Region it makes a fuller-bodied wine than its French relatives, but retains the fragrant bouquet and fruited flavor. Its quality is surpassed only by the Chardonnay and the true Riesling.

GRENACHE. A good quality, high-yield sweet grape producing wines high in alcohol with a distinctive bouquet. In France its best wines are the rosés of Tavel and the Rhône. It is blended in the Châteauneuf-du-Pape, and with a special vinification is made into the heavy, sweet Banyuls. In California it makes excellent rosés, usually labeled varietally, and superior grades of Port. It is planted extensively in the Rioja district of northern Spain.

BACO NO. 1. A French hybridizer, Maurice Baco, has given his name, followed by numerals and letters to a number of his creations. Baco No. 1 is being successfully grown in the U.S. Northeast, producing a very palatable, dark and robust red wine. It is usually labeled as "Baco Noir." It is quite popular with home wine makers and growers. In France **BACO NO. 22A** *(not shown),* a cross of Folle Blanche and Noah, is now used in making Armagnac brandy.

PALOMINO, or Golden Chasselas as it is known in California, is one of the finest table grapes. In Jerez it is the chief constituent of Sherry, but elsewhere in Spain it is used only for lesser, light wines. In California both light table wines and high-quality sherries are made from it. The wine has a delicate bouquet, but does not keep well because of the low acid content. Related varieties are the Gutedel of Germany and the Fendant of Switzerland.

OTHER IMPORTANT WINE GRAPES

ALIGOTÉ is a Burgundian white wine grape of secondary quality yielding an ordinary but quite agreeable *vin de carafe*. It is usually overpriced in the U.S.

BARBERA is a red wine grape of Piedmont, cultivated to some extent in California. There, as well as in its native Italy, it makes a deep-colored, robust, full-bodied wine which is at its best when quite young.

CATAWBA, a light-red grape, probably an accidental hybrid of wild American varieties, makes a white wine of pronounced labrusca flavor. It is grown extensively in the northeastern American regions for making champagne.

CHENIN BLANC is an excellent white wine grape, also known as Pineau de la Loire, and incorrectly as Pinot Blanc, or White Pinot, as it is not a true Pinot variety. In the French provinces of Touraine and Anjou it is the predominant grape, producing the Vouvray and Saumur wines. The early-maturing California varietal is a wine of great finesse and fine flavor.

CLAIRETTE. This good quality white wine grape is widely grown in the south of France, and to a lesser degree in California. Although white, it is blended into red Châteauneuf-du-Pape, and in rosés of Tavel; a delightful transformation.

DELAWARE is probably another accidental labrusca hybrid. It makes a fresh, pale, white wine with good balance and much less oppressive flavor than other labrusca wines. It is much used in Eastern U.S. champagnes, and in the best table wines of New York State, Ohio, and Canada.

ELVIRA is a native labrusca-riparia cross discovered toward the end of the nineteenth century in Missouri. The sizable plantings in the Finger Lakes Region of New York produce a fresh-tasting, very pleasant white wine of pronounced foxy flavor but considerable distinction.

FOLLE BLANCHE. This white wine grape is also known as Picpoul and Gros Plant in its native France. There are a number of plantings of this variety in northern California. It produces a clean-tasting light wine.

FURMINT is the famous fine white grape of Hungary, the principal ingredient of the renowned Tokay. It produces other fine Hungarian wines and is blended into some German wines.

GAMAY is the red grape of the popular French Beaujolais and of the fine California "Gamay du Beaujolais," which is not to be confused with an ordinary California wine of lesser quality sold as "Gamay."

GEWÜRZTRAMINER. This pinkish white wine grape of the Traminer family yields a rather soft, very heavily perfumed and spicy white wine in Alsace, where it is widely planted, and in Germany and Luxembourg. In California the wine retains all the true characteristics but is somewhat less spicy than its Old World counterpart.

GREEN HUNGARIAN is a California white wine grape of uncertain origin which yields a pleasant, light wine. Some of it is sold under its varietal name; the bulk is used in blending.

MERLOT is a fine red wine grape used to give softness and fruitiness to many Bordeaux and California clarets. It is seldom vinified alone, except in parts of northern Italy where it produces a soft, fragrant and very pleasant wine.

NEBBIOLO. This is Italy's outstanding red wine grape, responsible for the superb Barolo, Barbaresco, and Inferno. When fully matured its full-bodied wines have great distinction.

NIAGARA. One of the oldest American hybrids, this white wine grape is planted chiefly in the Finger Lakes Region of New York and in Canada. It makes a rather sweet, golden table wine of pronounced foxiness, very agreeable to those who appreciate the fragrance.

PEDRO XIMENEZ. This Spanish grape is thought to be the Rhine Valley's Riesling brought to Spain in the 16th century. In Malaga and the Sherry country it is vinified differently, producing the best sweetener for Sherry. In Montilla it is made into a fine dry wine. A sweet variety is drunk straight as a liqueur.

SANGIOVESE. This fine quality red wine grape of Italy is the principal (70%) constituent of Chianti, and in other regions of Italy it yields a very good but shorter-lived wine. In the tiny republic of San Marino it is served and consumed with great enjoyment. There are some plantings in California, but it is not used in the California Chiantis.

SCUPPERNONG. This is a unique American variety, a *Muscadine* grape of the sub-genus *Rotundifolia*. It is cultivated exclusively in the Carolinas for both table use and as a wine grape.

SÉMILLON is an excellent white wine grape of southwestern France where it is widely planted, and of California to a much smaller extent. It gives best results when vinified with another grape variety, particularly Sauvignon Blanc such as in Graves and Sauternes. It is generally most successful as a slightly sweet wine; when dry it has a tendency to bitterness especially when grown in warm regions.

SYLVANER is a very productive premium white wine grape grown extensively in such different parts of the world as Alsace, Austria, California, Chile, Germany, Italy, Luxembourg, and Switzerland. The wines it gives, usually labeled varietally, are light and pleasant. For some strange reason it can legally be called "Riesling" in California.

SYRAH, also spelled Sirah, is an excellent variety of red wine grape grown extensively in the Rhône Valley. It is the grape of the renowned Hermitage, and is one of the thirteen wines blended into Châteauneuf-du-Pape. Syrah is also grown in Australia, California, South Africa, and Switzerland. This superior quality grape should not be confused with **PETIT SYRAH** which makes a very satisfactory, full-bodied wine of less distinction. In California some vintners have made excellent varietals with Petit Syrah, but most of it is blended into "Burgundy."

TREBBIANO is an Italian white wine grape of many names, producing a pale, dry wine. In France it is called Ugni Blanc (*see below*) and some of it is grown in California. In Italy it is a constituent of White Chianti, and when blended with Malvasia it yields the sweet Orvieto, and Vin Santo.

UGNI BLANC (*see above*) has still another name in France, St. Émilion. Widely planted in the south of France, its best wine is that of Cassis. In California it finds its way into blends.

ZINFANDEL. This red wine grape of undetermined origin is an extensively planted variety in California. It is deservedly a very popular wine, fresh and pleasant with a distinctive "berry" flavor, the American counterpart to France's Beaujolais. It is widely blended.

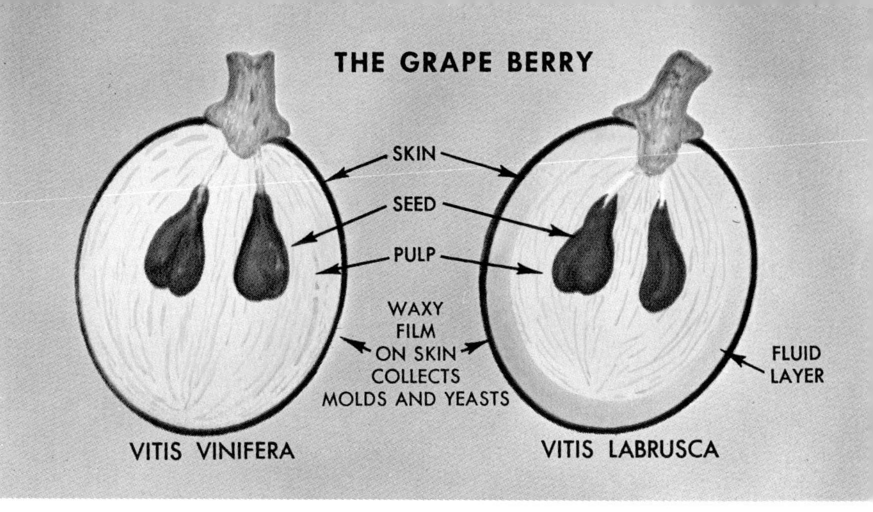

THE GRAPE BERRY is full of the juice and pulp containing the sugars, acids, tannins, aromatic compounds, minerals and even vitamins, all giving wine its unique character and quality. On the skin is a waxy layer, the frosty "bloom," whose function is to trap airborne yeasts and enzymes responsible for fermentation.

To make wine, all primitive man had to do was to break the skins allowing the wild yeasts to contact the sugary juice. It was Mother Nature's Self-Packaged Instant Mix. Fermentation took place and after a few days he could down a heady liquid unlike anything he had ever tasted. Overindulgence resulted in the condition known as "Stoned in the Bronze Age."

Man then learned to strain the unwanted skins, pulp, seeds, and anything else that may have fallen in his fermentation pot, obtaining a slightly turbid but more satisfying beverage. Later he mastered the art of storing it and, by trial and error, improved it until it reached the degree of excellence where poets would sing its praises. These refinements took centuries to achieve, and the search for perfection continues to this day.

THE BASIC STEPS TO WINE MAKING

The basic steps in the process of transforming grapes into wine are essentially the same in every wine-making region of the world.

The grapes are harvested at a given time and must arrive quickly and in good condition at the winery. They are crushed, their juice is fermented, the fermented juice is pressed, sediment is removed, the clarified wine is rested, aged, and eventually bottled.

While the above applies to the making of all still table wines, there are other steps in making special wines, such as Champagne, sparkling wines, sherry, and other fortified wines.

Techniques and equipment for these basic operations can, and do, vary from region to region, and from vintner to vintner. Some apply the latest technological advances in methods and use sophisticated equipment; others cling to time-honored procedures and equipment. Both can, and do, make good wine.

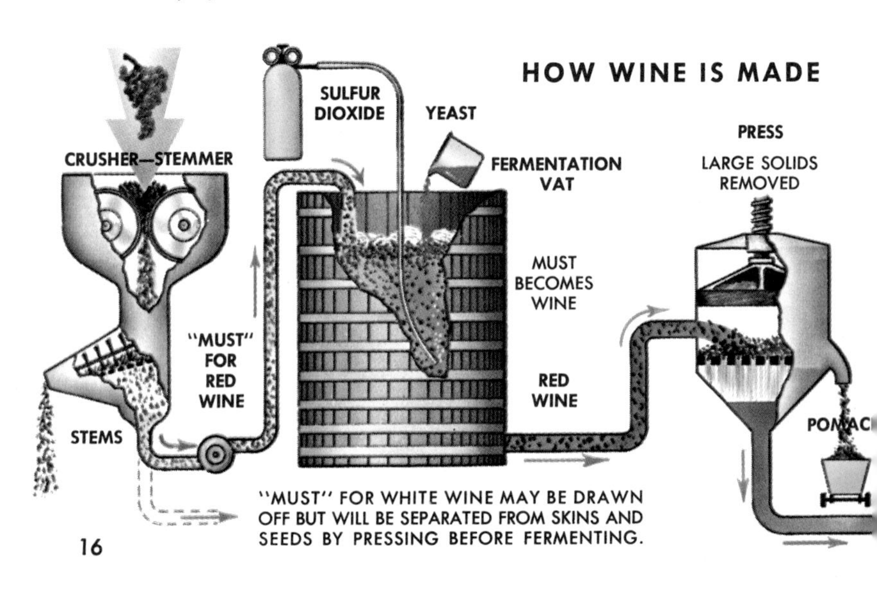

The red and gold leaves on the vines (*at right*) signal the approach of a busy harvest time in this California vineyard.

THE SCIENTIFIC APPROACH to wine making, leavened with some inherited intuitive traditional methods is typically American. The combination is being adopted gradually in many other parts of the world as new methods of viticulture and viniculture with new sophisticated equipment reach the furthest corners of the globe.

HARVESTING begins when the vineyardist determines that the grapes have reached the precise ripeness for the type of wine to be made. He makes periodic laboratory tests for sugar contents and acidity as well as the traditional checks with sight, feel, and taste during the growing season. The vine and its fruit are constantly under his watchful eye.

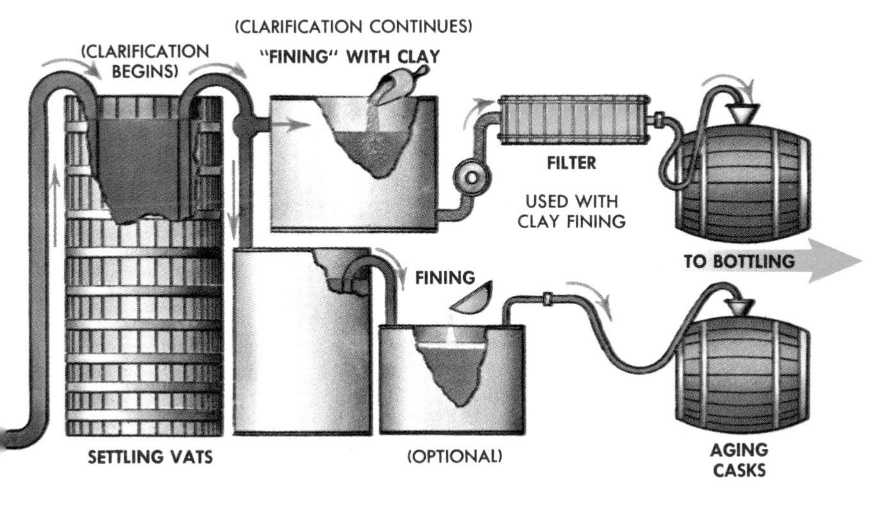

PICKING the grapes is still very much of a hand operation in most of the world's vineyards. The varieties from which the finest wines are made are usually thin-skinned and must not be bruised or broken before they arrive at the crushers. The work of a grape picker requires speed, a certain amount of manual dexterity, and a strong back.

Large numbers of pickers are necessary to do the job quickly, for a relatively short period of employment. The labor problem, with its attending economic complexities, has become increasingly difficult to solve where great industrial growth and urbanization are on the rise.

MECHANICAL HARVESTERS may be part of the solution. These machines may be in common use in the near future, mechanizing the picking as tractors mechanized the plowing and cultivating. A number of harvesters are now in use in New York State and California.

The machine requires a special spacing of the rows of vines and a different supporting trellis. The newly planted vineyards in California, New York, and other parts of the United States are being laid out to accommodate the giant machines.

The mechanical harvesters seen from the front and rear in the pictures at left are operating in a Taylor vineyard. The berries are gently shaken loose from the vine and conveyed directly to a tractor-drawn gondola in the adjoining row.

TRANSPORTING the grapes to the crusher requires a strong back and sure foot on the very steep slopes of some hillside vineyards, such as those of the Rheingau and the Rhône.

The picker's harvest is collected in back-baskets and carried to level ground where it is transferred to animal-drawn carts. Where the ground is level and modern technology applied, tractor-drawn gondolas circulate through the rows collecting the accumulation.

INSPECTION takes place at the winery. The grapes are weighed, and an on-the-spot test of their sugar content is taken to determine the price for those supplied by outside vineyards. The grapes are then unloaded, washed, and conveyed to a stemmer, a machine which can separate 20 tons of berries from their stems in one hour. The stems are pulverized and plowed into the vineyard soil as mulch and organic fertilizer.

THE IDEAL LOCATION for a winery is on a hillside, with the grapes arriving at the highest level, and the presses and fermenting tanks on successive levels below. The processing of the grapes and their juice can then be effected, or aided by gravity, avoiding pumping as much as possible.

Where the land is too flat to permit the use of gravity as a transporting force, belt conveyors are used to move the grapes, and pumps to move the juice from the presses to the tanks.

CRUSHING follows the removal of stems, or is done simultaneously in a crusher-stemmer. Crushing converts the berries into a pulpy mass called "must."

SULFURING, the next step, consisted in the old method of burning sulfur candles in the casks to produce sulfur dioxide. Today the sterilizing gas is added to the must in precise amounts from metal cylinders. Sulfur dioxide controls unwanted microorganisms, inhibits the browning effect of enzymes, and retards oxidation.

PRESSING extracts the juice from the grapes. Many types of presses are used, from the familiar ancient slotted wooden basket with screw-operated piston to ingenious equipment such as the Willmes bladder press, effectively separating the juice from the solids, called "pomace," consisting mainly of skins, seeds, and pulp.

This press, whose slotted sides are too small to pass skins and seeds, contains an air-inflatable rubber bag which squeezes the must against the sides. The juice is drained off at the bottom and the dry pomace expelled before the operation is repeated.

RED WINE derives its color from the grape skins whose pigments gradually dissolve into the fermenting must. Other desirable characteristics of red wine are derived from the other solids.

FOR WHITE WINE to be produced the juice must be separated from the pomace *before* fermentation by pressing. This avoids color and taste characteristics unwanted in white wine. Only the juice is fermented.

Traditional oak open-top fermentation tanks in use at the Pleasant Valley Wine Company, New York *(above)*.

The newest in jacketed stainless steel tanks (*left*). In the favorable climates of Australia and California, some vintners install the tanks outdoors.

Giant glass-lined steel tanks, each holding 100,000 gallons of wine, in use at the Taylor winery, New York *(below)*.

SEPARATION of fluid from solids occurs during the fermentation of red wine. It is possible to drain off about 2/3rds of the wine from settling tanks. This portion is called "*free-run*" as opposed to "*press-run,*" when the remaining portion is pressed. The end portion of the pressing is less desirable and may be sold as lower grade wine, distilled for its alcohol, or used in blending.

FERMENTATION becomes quite active within about 12 hours and stops automatically when practically all the sugar has been converted to alcohol, usually a maximum of 14 to 15% alcohol by volume. It can be stopped by the wine maker in a number of ways.

For controlled fermentation a selected wine yeast is added to the sulfured must and thoroughly mixed. Heat is generated during fermentation but must not be allowed to reach a temperature slowing the yeast's action to the point where fermentation stops. A "stuck" fermentation can be a real disaster. Small fermentation containers are less likely to overheat than the big tanks of the large wineries. Cooling devices such as heat exchangers and immersion coils may be used to control the heat and rate of fermentation.

FERMENTING TANKS, large or small, are filled from ½ to ¾ capacity to allow for expansion and the accumulation of foam caused by the large volume of carbon dioxide gas produced.

Specially designed jacketed stainless steel tanks with precise automatic temperature controls are in use in warm regions. Elsewhere different methods are used to control the rate and heat of fermentation. Pressurized fermentors are favored in Germany, while in Champagne and Burgundy fermentation rooms are sometimes heated when the weather turns cold during the vintage season.

Fermenting red wine is 'pumped over' the hard crust of pomace that has been pushed to the top of the fermentation vat by the escaping carbon dioxide gas.

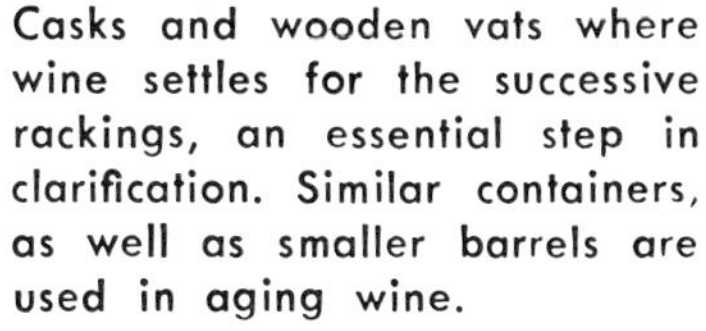

Casks and wooden vats where wine settles for the successive rackings, an essential step in clarification. Similar containers, as well as smaller barrels are used in aging wine.

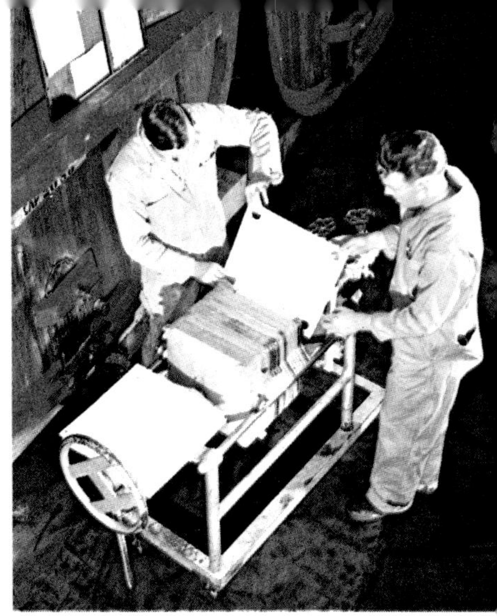

Filter pads are inserted between filter plates to catch suspended sediment, a step in the process of clarification. Not all wines are filtered; some are racked several times, and then bottled.

CLARIFICATION begins after fermentation is completed, or has been stopped. The pomace is separated from the turbid fluid which stands until a large portion of the fine suspended material, mostly yeast cells, collects at the bottom of the settling tank as *lees*.

RACKING now begins. In this universally used process the relatively clear wine is carefully drawn off by siphoning or pumping without stirring up the lees. The process is repeated several times, some vintners going no further than racking to clarify their wine. Clarity, particularly in America, is a quality criterion. Some vintners fine and filter as well as rack.

FINING is a traditional method of clarifying wine through the use of a variety of substances such as egg whites, isinglass, casein, and special types of clays, notably *Bentonite*.

The fining medium is added to the previously racked wine. It settles to the bottom carrying with it the fine suspended particles. With clays, filtering is usually required.

This automatic, high-speed bottling machine fills more than a dozen bottles at once.

BOTTLING the wine is an almost completely automated process, not only in the highly mechanized wineries of the U.S., but in all wine-growing regions of the world. These machines have made the large winery possible since filling, labeling and packing the millions of bottles by hand would be an endless task.

AGING RED WINES begins at the winery, but continues until the cork is pulled. Depending on the type and quality, the wine remains in aging casks for a period ranging from weeks to years. A relatively large number of vintners producing high quality red wines age their bottled stock an additional year or more.

Winery workers place decorative and protective lead foil capsules on newly-corked bottles. Labels will be added, mostly by machine, in these, the latter stages of processing the wine to the consumer.

Machine labeling, some hand labeling, and the final inspection *(above left)*. Additional bottle-aging in the carefully temperature-controlled winery warehouse *(above right)*.

BOTTLE-AGING is a prerogative of the consumer. A fine red wine, purchased as soon as available and kept in a suitable "wine cellar" should improve and grow in value until it reaches full maturity. A good wine cellar is within the scope of a modest budget, and buying wine for storage will be discussed later on.

This California varietal wine, a Pinot Blanc, reaches its final destination: gracing the host's table. Properly chilled, it will add to the enjoyment of the wine-poached shrimp it accompanies.

We live in an age where old-fashioned craftsmanship and identification of the maker with his product is rapidly disappearing from many professions. One which has, to a large extent, avoided this depersonalization is that of the wine maker.

Throughout the world wine makers continue to identify with their delightful product, proudly signing their name to the label as an artist signs his canvas proclaiming: "This is *my* work." More often than not it is a hereditary profession, particularly with the smaller vineyards, passed on from father to sons, generation after generation.

The infinite variety of wines produced is all based on growing vines to produce good crops of grapes, fermenting the juice and skillfully nursing the wine until it is ready to bottle for the consumer.

In the climate belts of both the northern and southern hemispheres, where the grape vine grows, the wine makers' prime concerns are the weather and the character of the soil. They must select the grape that will make the best wine under these two conditions over which they have no effective control. The Europeans, after centuries of trial and error, have settled on the varieties best suited for each region but in the relatively new wine worlds of America and Australia the ideal combinations are now being found with a strong assist from improved scientific viticultural methods.

Wine makers' methods vary to some extent from region to region, but the basic procedure remains the same. The shiny new equipment is usually only a labor-saving refinement of the traditional device. Centrifuges, ion-exchangers and rotating fermentation tanks are definitely innovations, but these are still somewhat experimental and not yet in general use.

We shall see, in the pages that follow, the wide varieties of wines that are made, their characteristics, and the methods used to make them.

THE UNITED STATES

The history of wine in the New World begins with the explorers. There is no evidence that the Indians made wine from any of the wild grapes growing in their territories. The abundance of wild grapes found by Lief Ericson and his shipmates caused them to name their discovery "Vineland," but it was left to the later settlers to cultivate the native vine and make the first American wine from its berries. Judging from old records of the colonists it was quite a poor and unrewarding beverage. Columbus brought his own wine, mostly Sherry, in his ships, and the missionary monks who accompanied the later Conquistadores brought the European grape vine with them. They planted their vineyards as they established their chain of missions northward from Mexico along the Pacific coast.

The new settlers were eager to make wine wherever they established their new homes, some with the native grape, and some with the transplanted European vines. In the East the harsh winters quickly destroyed the imported vines, unused to the extreme cold, but the same *Vitis vinifera* flourished happily in what is now California. For many years the settlers in the East and Canada cultivated and improved the native *Vitis labrusca,* the only vine variety which successfully withstood the rigors of the climate. William Penn's gardener, John Alexander, is credited with the earliest American hybrid which bears his name. His success in creating a viable variety capable of making palatable wine greatly encouraged others to develop the Elvira, Concord, Catawba, Delaware, and a few other early crossings still very popular in Ohio, New York State and Canada.

Until recently the per capita wine consumption in America was so low that it was not considered a wine-drinking country. Over the past few decades the increase has been spectacularly rapid, as evidenced by the total quantity (in round figures) of commercially produced wine entering U.S. distribution channels:

100 million gallons in the period just after WW II
150 million gallons (average) through the 1950's
200 million gallons (average) through the 1960's
250 million gallons by 1970
400 million gallons (estimated) by 1980

By 1969 the U.S. had risen to seventh place in world production of wine, with Italy first, France second, and Spain third. Within the next decade it is likely that it will move up another place.

As consumption increases, Americans are becoming more knowledgeable and discriminating by forming tasting clubs and joining such consumer-oriented groups as the American Wine Society.

The famous American author, Washington Irving, was a great and discriminating connoisseur. His wine cellar was famed among his friends who were entertained at his charming home, "Sunnyside," on the banks of the Hudson River at Irvington, N.Y.

CALIFORNIA

California's fertile valleys and slopes provide an ideal setting for grape cultivation. The climate even permits open-air wineries in some locations. While the grape can be grown in most of the state's 58 counties, the principal wine areas are: the cool Northern Coastal Region around San Francisco, producing mostly table wines; the much warmer Great Inland Valley Region where, until recently, the emphasis was on fortified wines; and the Southern Region, reaching eastward from Los Angeles, producing wines which compare favorably with those of the French Midi.

The history of California wines begins with the chain of missions and their adjoining vineyards, established in the latter part of the 18th Century by the Franciscan monks. Eventually the chain reached from the Mexican border to Sonoma. Later, other European immigrants brought their wine making skills and other varieties of *Vitis vinifera* to the new land of wine. Colonel Agoston Haraszthy, in 1861, brought some two hundred thousand vines and cuttings he collected from the famous European vineyards. His experimental plantings made a substantial improvement throughout the state and deservedly earned him the title of "Father of California's modern wine industry."

On the map, *opposite,* the principal wine growing regions are shown in red. The Northern Coastal Region, from Ukiah to Soledad, is cooled by Pacific breezes. The Great Inland Valley, cradled between the Coast Range and the Sierra Nevada, extends from north of Sacramento to Bakersfield. The Southern Region, from Ventura to Escondido, includes the Los Angeles and Cucamonga districts.

Vineyard Districts of California
UKIAH
OROVILLE
ASTI
ST. HELENA
SANTA ROSA
RUTHERFORD
NAPA
SONOMA
Lake Tahoe
SACRAMENTO
LODI
SAN FRANCISCO
LIVERMORE
MISSION SAN JOSE
MODESTO
SANTA CLARA
SAN MARTIN
SAN JUAN BAUTISTA
PAICINES
MADERA
FRESNO
SOLEDAD
HANFORD
TULARE
PASO ROBLES
TEMPLETON
BAKERSFIELD
VENTURE
Pacific Ocean
CUCAMONGA
SAN BERNARDINO
GUASTI
Los Angeles
WHITTIER
SAN MARCOS
ESCONDIDO
San Diego

The mid-eighteen hundreds saw the founding of many wineries operating today, some under the direction of the founder's descendants. To name but a few: Mirassou, Almadén, and Paul Masson in Santa Clara; Schramsberg in Calistoga; Charles Krug, The Christian Brothers, Beringer Brothers, and Inglenook in Napa; the Italian-Swiss Colony, and Korbel in Sonoma; Wente, and Concannon in Alameda; and in 1900, the founding of Beaulieu Vineyards in Napa.

A number of near disasters plagued the industry; first, the phylloxera attacked the European vines but the discovery that grafting the *Vitis vinifera* onto the native *Vitis labrusca* rootstock avoided a complete decimation; then two wine depressions caused by overplanting and production of poor quality wine severely damaged the reputation of the wines. The crushing blow came with the Eighteenth Amendment. Grape production was maintained to provide grapes for home wine makers, sacramental wine production and a few other uses still permitted by the "dry laws."

These unhappy times for California vintners ended with Repeal. Working in cooperation with both state and federal governments they rebuilt their great industry on a sound basis.

The California wine regions are far and away the largest producers in the United States. During the early years of the rebirth, following Repeal, about 75% of the wines were dessert or fortified wines, the remaining 25% divided between table wines and sparkling wines. The proportion has changed radically in the past few decades so that by 1970 table wines had outstripped dessert wines by more than 40 million gallons. This is a strong indication of the serious interest in American table wines as an integral part of a meal.

Unlike their European counterparts most California wineries made as many different types of wines as possible. The result was, too often, great variety at the cost of indifferent or inferior quality. A reversal of this policy is gaining popularity, particularly with some of the smaller growers who are limiting their production to two or three outstanding wines instead of the former assortment of a dozen or more types. The larger growers may be following suit as their extensive recent plantings of premium varieties come to maturity. The most recent plantings, both large and small, have been chiefly of the grapes which produce the superb varietals such as Cabernet Sauvignon. Careful scientific studies of soil and climate have enabled growers to plant the premium varieties best suited for their location.

The number of high quality California wines is increasing every year, and the amount produced is also growing significantly. While some are difficult to obtain outside of California, the hope is that increased production will remedy this situation.

THE SONOMA-MENDOCINO, NAPA-SOLANO DISTRICTS rank high in the number of bonded wineries, producing vast quantities of good standard quality table wines, principally reds, and a number of top quality premium wines and champagnes. A partial listing of its wineries follows:

BEAULIEU VINEYARD was founded in 1900 by Georges de Latour. All its wines are marketed under the *Beaulieu Vineyard (BV)* label, and bear the Napa Valley appellation of origin. Almost all are estate bottled and the back label states exactly what grapes have been used. The varietals are usually 100% of the grapes named.
Red Table Wines: Cabernet Sauvignon and Cabernet Sauvignon Private Reserve, Beaumont Pinot Noir, and Burgundy.
White Table Wines: Beaufort Pinot Chardonnay, Beauclair Johannisberg Riesling, Dry and Sweet Sauterne, Chablis, and Riesling.
Rosé Table Wines: Beaurosé, and Grenache Rosé.
Sparkling Wines: Private Reserve Champagne *Brut,* BV Champagne *Brut* and *Extra Dry,* and *Rouge* (Sparkling Burgundy).
Aperitif and Dessert Wines: Sherries, Port, and Muscat de Frontignan.

BERINGER BROTHERS, INC., was founded in 1876 by two brothers, Jacob and Frederick Beringer. To insure uniform character and quality Beringer wines are well aged and blended. They are now concentrating on varietals. Beringer "Private Stock," is the featured brand.
Red Table Wines: Barenblut (Blood of the Bear), a house specialty, Cabernet Sauvignon, Grignolino, Pinot Noir, Zinfandel, and Burgundy.
White Table Wines: Dry and Sweet Sauterne, Johannisberg Riesling, Grey Riesling, Chenin Blanc, Sauvignon Blanc, and Chardonnay. Beringer makes the usual aperitif and dessert wines, and a specialty, Malvasia Bianca. They also feature Brut Champagne, Pink Champagne, Sparkling Burgundy and Beringer Bros. Brandy.

BUENA VISTA VINEYARDS was once the home of Agoston Haraszthy, the Hungarian nobleman credited with starting modern California viticulture. In 1861 he collected over 300 grape varieties in Europe and planted them here. A series of disasters haunted the vineyard and its owners until 1943 when it was revived, and now markets its premium wines under the Buena Vista label.

Red Table Wines: Cabernet Sauvignon (Estate Bottled), Pinot Noir, Zinfandel (which grew to fame in this vineyard), and Burgundy.
White Table Wines: Pinot Chardonnay, White Riesling Johannisberg, Traminer, Sylvaner, Grey Riesling (all Estate Bottled), Sonoma Semillon, Green Hungarian (a specialty), Chablis, and Vine Brook (from Sylvaner grapes). Two rosés are made, Rosé Brook (Estate Bottled, from Cabernet Sauvignon grapes), and Grenache Rosé.

A bottle fermented, Estate grown Pinot Chardonnay Champagne *Brut* is also made, as well as Sherry and Vintage Port.

CHAPPELLET WINERY, one of the newest in the region, was established by Donn Chappellet in 1969. The pyramid-shaped winery houses the gleaming modern equipment and traditional aging barrels for the premium varietals made from the estate's own plantings. Production is limited to the types best suited for the area surrounding the winery. The plantings are restricted to such varietals as Cabernet Sauvignon, Chenin Blanc, and Riesling.

THE CHRISTIAN BROTHERS, a Roman Catholic teaching order, started their California wine making operations in 1882. Their extensive plantings and wineries in the Napa Valley enable them to produce great quantities and varieties of premium wines, as well as special sacramental wines.

The Brothers do not vintage their wines, preferring to blend for uniform high quality. Their bulk wines, in gallons and half-gallons, are exactly the same quality as the wine bottled in fifths and smaller containers.

The bulk of the Brothers' wines and brandy are sold under *The Christian Brothers* label, except the sacramental wines which are bottled under the *Mont La Salle* brand. The Brothers supervise all activities at their wineries from the growing to the final bottling.

The varietals include:
Red Table Wine: Cabernet Sauvignon, Gamay, Pinot Noir, and Pinot St. George.
White Table Wines: Dry and Sweet Sauvignon Blanc and Semillon, Pinot Chardonnay, Chenin Blanc, Johannisberg Riesling, Riesling, Sylvaner, Grey Riesling, and Chateau La Salle, a light muscat. The usual assortment of premium generics such as Burgundy, Sauterne and Chablis are also made.

HEITZ WINE CELLARS is owned by Joseph and Alice Heitz. Using their extensive knowledge of wine, they select, blend, mature and bottle other producers' wines and sell them under their own label.
Red Table Wines: Barbera, Burgundy, Cabernet Sauvignon, Grignolino, Pinot Noir, and Ruby Cabernet.
White Table Wines: Chablis, Johannisberg Riesling, and Pinot Blanc. The above are sold under the *Heitz Cellar* label, under their *Cellar Treasure* label a Tawny Port and an Angelica.

INGLENOOK, an old stone winery, is a Napa Valley showplace built in 1879. It was the first winery to label varietals as such. All the wines are

marked with the vintage year; some carry the cask number.
Red Table Wines: Cabernet Sauvignon, Pinot Noir, Pinot St. George, Gamay, Zinfandel, and Charbono.
White Table Wines: Grey Riesling, White Pinot, Traminer, Pinot Chardonnay, Sylvaner, Johannisberg Riesling, Chenin Blanc, Riesling, Dry Semillon.

Inglenook also makes Navalle Rosé, Vintage Champagne and dessert and appetizer wines.

ITALIAN SWISS COLONY, founded in 1881 is now one of the giants of the wine industry, a cooperative producing as much as 25% of U.S. volume.

The bulk of its production is in medium priced wines of good quality, but it also markets some premium wines under its *Private Stock* label. Generic wines are sold under the *Tipo* brand.

The usual assortment of table, aperitif, and dessert wines are marketed under the *Gold Medal Reserve* and *Private Stock* labels. The Italian Swiss Colony is now part of the giant combine under United Vintners, Inc.

F. KORBEL & BROS. is the home of champagnes rated among the best in the country. The original winery was built in 1886. Marketed under the *Korbel* brand are: Korbel Nature (very dry), Korbel Brut (dry), Korbel Extra Dry and Korbel Sec (both medium dry), Korbel Rouge, and Korbel Rosé. The table wines include: Chablis, Sauterne, Grey Riesling, Rosé, Burgundy, Cabernet, and Pinot Noir.

CHARLES KRUG WINERY, dating back to 1861, is now run by the Mondavi family and has been completely modernized. The main accent is on premium table wines, sold under the *Charles Krug* label, with less expensive wines sold under the *CK* and *Mondavi Vintage* labels. Besides the usual generic wines the following varietals are made:

Red Table Wines: Cabernet Sauvignon, Gamay, Pinot Noir, and Mountain Zinfandel.

White Table Wines: Dry, and Sweet Semillon, Sweet Sauvignon Blanc, White Pinot, Chenin Blanc, Pinot Chardonnay, Traminer, Gewurztraminer, Sylvaner, Grey Riesling and Johannisberg Riesling.

LOUIS M. MARTINI wines are among California's best.

Red Table Wines: Vintage Cabernet Sauvignon and Vintage Mountain Pinot Noir. Also, Barbera and Zinfandel.

White Table Wines: Johannisberg Riesling, Mountain Gewurztraminer, Mountain Sylvaner, Mountain Folle Blanche, and Mountain Dry Semillon. All are Vintage.

Also: Mountain Riesling, Mountain Dry Chenin Blanc, and Mountain Pinot Chardonnay.

A number of generic table wines, two rosés, and four aperitif and dessert wines are also produced. Available only at the winery are some special vintage table wines and an effervescent Moscato Amabile.

MAYACAMAS VINEYARDS are located on top of Mt. Veeder, an extinct volcano. The relatively small winery produces some outstanding wines, under the *Mayacamas* label, all 100% of the variety shown on the label. Production has been limited to a few varieties grown on the estate, Cabernet Sauvignon, Pinot Chardonnay, Chenin Blanc, and Zinfandel.

ROBERT MONDAVI WINERY was started in 1966 by Robert Mondavi and his son to produce the finest Napa Valley wines possible. The grapes are purchased from other growers and vinified by a judicious use of innovative and traditional methods. All the wines produced are varietals.

Red Table Wines: Cabernet Sauvignon, Gamay, Pinot Noir, and Zinfandel.

White Table Wines: Chardonnay, Chenin Blanc, Fumé Blanc, Riesling, Sauvignon Blanc, and Traminer.

SCHRAMSBERG VINEYARDS, made famous in literature by Robert Louis Stevenson is now producing only premium quality bottle fermented sparkling wines. The vineyards have been replanted in Pinot Noir and Chardonnay, the principal varieties used to make the French Champagnes.
Blanc de Blancs—a blend of Chardonnay and Pinot Blanc.
Cuvée de Gamay—A light, pink sparkling Napa Gamay wine.
Blanc de Noir—A white Champagne made of Pinot Noir grapes.

SAMUELE SEBASTIANI is the oldest winery in Sonoma Valley operated continuously by one family. In 1954 the son of the founder decided to change the operation from production of bulk wine to premium varieties. Under the *Sebastiani* label are produced table wines, aperitif, dessert wines and vermouths, as well as bottle-fermented sparkling wines. Featured wines include: Barbera, Cabernet Sauvignon, Gamay Beaujolais, Pinot Noir, and Green Hungarian.

SOUVERAIN CELLARS, founded in 1943 by J. Leland Stewart have successfully achieved the aim to blend the best old-world traditions with the latest modern California methods of winemaking. Wines marketed under the *Souverain* brand include:
Red Table Wines: Burgundy, Cabernet Sauvignon, Petite Sirah, and Mountain Zinfandel.
White Table Wines: Johannisberg Riesling, White Pinot, Green Hungarian, Chenin Blanc, Flora, and Chardonnay.
There is also a Grenache Rosé.

THE ALAMEDA, CONTRA COSTA, and **SANTA CLARA, SANTA CRUZ, SAN BENITO DISTRICTS** include the celebrated *Livermore Valley* where the finest California Sauterne-type wines are produced, the equally famous Alameda region around *Mission San Jose,* and the great vineyards of Almadén and Paul Masson.

ALMADÉN VINEYARDS is one of the giants of California. The Paicines and Valliant plantings alone cover more than 4,000 acres. The storage sheds at Paicines hold about 60 million gallons of wine. Its bigness does not detract from quality as the complete selection of premium wines marketed under the *Almadén* label attests.

Red Table Wines: Cabernet Sauvignon, Pinot Noir, Gamay Beaujolais, generics such as Mountain reds, and Estate-Bottled Vintage varietals.
White Table Wines: Pinot Chardonnay, Pinot Blanc, Johannisberg Riesling, Dry Semillon, Traminer, Sylvaner, Grey Riesling, Chenin Blanc, Sauvignon Blanc and white generics.

CONCANNON VINEYARD was founded in 1883 by James Concannon, and is still run by his descendants. Here the emphasis is on Johannisberg Riesling, Petite Sirah, and Cabernet Sauvignon. Top quality generics and varietals are produced, as well as aperitif, dessert and bottle-fermented sparkling wines.
Red Table Wines: Cabernet Sauvignon, Petite Sirah, Livermore Red Dinner Wine.
White Table Wines: Sauvignon Blanc, Johannisberg Riesling, Dry Sauterne, Chateau Concannon, Chablis, Moselle, and Livermore White Dinner Wine.

LLORDS & ELWOOD WINERY, built in 1955, uses proprietary names for its varietals.
Red Table Wines: Cabernet Sauvignon, Velvet Hill (Pinot Noir).
White Table Wines: Castle Magic (Johannisberg Riesling), and The Rare Chardonnay.
Sherries: Great Day D-r-r-y Sherry, Dry Wit Sherry, and The Judge's Secret Cream Sherry.
Port: Ancient Proverb Port.
Rosé: Rosé of Cabernet.

CRESTA BLANCA winery, built in 1883, features white wines from Livermore Valley and reds from Napa and Sonoma.
Red Table Wines: Cabernet Sauvignon, Pinot Noir, Zinfandel, Petite Sirah, Gamay Beaujolais, Grignolino, and Mountain Burgundy.
White Table Wines: Pinot Chardonnay, Grey Riesling, French Colombard, Dry Semillon, Green Hungarian, Sauterne, and Mountain Chablis.
Rosé: Grenache Rosé

There are also Dessert, Cocktail, and Sparkling Wines.

PAUL MASSON is a great name in the history of California wine. Establishing his first vineyard in 1852, the young Burgundian who gave his name to the company won a gold medal for his wine in Paris in 1900.

Recent expansions and extensive plantings such as the 330-acre San Ysidro Vineyard, and the 1,500-acre Pinnacles Vineyard have assured its place as one of the largest wine makers.

Paul Masson produces a complete gamut of generic and varietal table wines, sparkling, aperitif, dessert wines, vermouths and brandies.

The varietals include:
Red Table Wines: Cabernet Sauvignon, Gamay Beaujolais and Pinot Noir. Two proprietary reds of special merit are the *Baroque*, a Burgundy type, and *Rubion*, a ready-to-drink claret blend.
White Table Wines: Pinot Blanc, Pinot Chardonnay, Chateau Masson (Sweet Semillon), and Emerald Dry.

MIRASSOU VINEYARDS: The fifth generation of Mirassous is now running this unusual operation. Originally the vineyards produced premium quality varietal wine and champagne stock for sale to other wineries. Now an increasing proportion of the harvest is made into wine under the *Mirassou* label. The Mirassou varietals are bottled at approximately 100% from the named varietal, far exceeding the legal requirement of 51% minimum.
Red Table Wines: Petite Sirah, Pinot Noir, Cabernet Sauvignon, Gamay Beaujolais, Zinfandel.
White Table Wines: Pinot Blanc, Chardonnay, White Riesling, Chenin Blanc, Gewürztraminer, Sauvignon Blanc, Riesling, Sylvaner, and Sémillon. A Grenache Rosé and sparkling wines, bottle-fermented are also bottled under their label.

MARTIN RAY, a successful stockbroker, realized his ambition to become a wine maker in 1936. He and his son have devoted their skills to the production of fine table wines and champagnes. The wines are all 100% varietal. Two red table wines made are *Pinot Noir* and *Cabernet Sauvignon. Chardonnay* is the only white. The bottle fermented champagnes are: *Madame Pinot,* a blanc de noir made from free run juice; *Blanc de Noir,* the costliest Martin Ray champagne; *Sang de Pinot; Champagne de Chardonnay,* a blanc de blancs.

SAN MARTIN VINEYARDS CO. was founded in 1932 by Bruno Filice. A full selection of table wines, sparkling wines, aperitif, dessert wines, vermouths and fruit wines is marketed under the *San Martin* and *Castlewood* labels:
Red Table Wines: Cabernet Sauvignon, Cabernet Ruby, Gamay Beaujolais, Pinot Noir, and Zinfandel.
White Table Wines: Pinot Chardonnay, Dry Sémillon, Sylvaner Riesling, Emerald Riesling, and Malvasia Bianca.

Generics include a Mountain Grenache Rosé Chianti.

WEIBEL, INC., founded in 1939, is famous for its champagnes, and produces premium table, aperitif, and dessert wines.

Champagnes: Bottle-fermented Chardonnay Brut, Extra Dry, Sec, Pink Champagne and Sparkling Burgundy. Also Crackling Rosé and Moscato Spumante.
Red Table Wines: Pinot Noir, Cabernet Sauvignon, Royalty, Zinfandel. Also red generics.
White Table Wines: Chardonnay, Johannisberg Riesling, Chenin Blanc, Green Hungarian, and Grey Riesling, plus white generics. A Grenache Rosé is available, also Vintage Pinot Noir and Chardonnay.

A specialty, *Tangor,* has the flavor of tangerines.

WENTE BROS. is one of the great names in the history of California wines. Carl H. Wente, the founder, built his first winery in 1883. The gravelly vineyards are well suited to the fine varieties planted there. The Wentes produce only table wines. Their white wines, in the opinion of many experts, are unsurpassed in California. Almost all their varietals carry the vintage date.
White Table Wines: Pinot Chardonnay, Pinot Blanc, Chablis, Dry Sémillon, Sauvignon Blanc, Chateau Wente, a blend, Grey Riesling, and Le Blanc des Blancs, made of Chenin Blanc and Ugni.
Red Table Wines: Burgundy, Pinot Noir, Gamay Beaujolais, and Rosé.

THE GREAT INLAND VALLEY and **SOUTHERN CALIFORNIA REGIONS** have the climate and soil that produce the great California aperitif and dessert wines as well as many of the other varieties. It includes the districts of *Lodi-Sacramento, Escalon-Modesto, Fresno-San Joaquin Valley, Cucamonga,* and *Los Angeles.*

BROOKSIDE VINEYARD CO., founded in 1832 is still operated by the Biane family. They operate 28 wine cellars where sales are made directly to the consumer.

Brookside pioneered the branch winery sales tasting cellar concept. They offer a choice of all types of wines: over a dozen *Brookside Estate* wines; nine Vaché wines, twenty-odd *Assumption Abbey* wines; as many under the *Brookside Cellar* label, and sparkling wines, sherries, brandies, etc.

CUCAMONGA WINERY claims the honor of being the first with the Cucamonga name. It produces only red and white table wines, and vermouths, a distinction in an area where great variety is the rule. They are all of premium quality and are distributed in the East and Midwest.

Under the featured brand *Romano Cucamonga* are the usual generic wines, Chianti, Dry Muscat and red varietals including: Barbera, Grignolino, and Zinfandel.

E. & J. GALLO WINERY is perhaps the best-known name among California brands. It is also one of the biggest operations in the state. The Gallo brothers believe that Americans want wines made to their taste, that it must be inexpensive, and that the product should be vigorously advertised. They founded their winery and have acted on their philosophy, building their company to giant size. They market some forty types of wines, some traditional such as the popular generics, some specially blended for "the American taste" including completely innovative types such as the "pop" wines. While there are many who deplore the Gallo products and philosophy, they have contributed and continue to contribute to the popularization of wine in America.

GUILD WINE COMPANY, formerly known as "*Wine Growers Guild,*" is a federation of cooperative wineries representing about 1,000 members, 9 major wine brands, 6 sparkling wine brands, and 5 brandies. All are bottled in Lodi, but are made at wineries in Ukiah, Woodbridge, Fresno, Guasti, and Lodi.

The handsome *Winemasters Guild* label, adopted in the early 70's, may unify some of the multitude of brands produced by the Guild. These include: *Tavola, Ceremony, Famiglia Cribari, Mendocino, Garrett, Alta, C.V.C.,* and *Virginia Dare*.

PETRI WINERIES are a part of the super-giant United Vintners, marketing arm of Allied Grape Growers, a cooperative with 1,800 members. Brands include G&D, Italian Swiss Colony, Petri, Mission Bell, Greystone, Cella, and many others.

The *Petri* label is found on the regular table, dessert, and aperitif wines. *Marca Petri* is used for the *Vino Rosso Pastoso,* a mellow Italian-type table wine.

ROMA WINE COMPANY, founded in 1890, expanded to giant size in the 1930's. The winery areas alone exceed 50 acres, and can store 25 million gallons.

Roma wines are sound standard quality, marketed nationally and exported under various brands such as *Roma Reserve, Roma Estate, and Roma Select.*

Almost all Roma aperitif and dessert wines are made from grapes grown in the San Joaquin Valley. Table wines include: *Vino d'Uva, Vino Bianco, Barberone, Chianti,* and *Zinfandel,* all under the *Roma Pride of the Vineyard* label.

READING A CALIFORNIA WINE LABEL

AMERICAN WINE LABELS are clear and explicit. Most of the information is strictly prescribed by law, just as is the case with many of their foreign counterparts. The California labels exemplify "truth in labeling."

1. *Name of the Maker*—The reputation of the maker rides on this identification.
2. *Vintage*—95% of the wine *must* have been produced in the year stated.
3. *Origin*—No identification of origin is allowed unless at least 75% of the wine comes from grapes grown and fermented in the designated region.
4. *Alcoholic Content*—Statement required by law. Table and sparkling wines contain 10 to 14% alcohol by volume; aperitif and dessert wines contain 17 to 20%.
5. *Produced and Bottled by . . .*—Possibly the most important statement. "*Estate Bottled*" indicates wine is made from grapes grown in a vineyard owned or controlled, and in the vicinity of the winery.

If the word "*Made*" is used, it can mean that as much as 90% may have been produced by others.

If "*Estate Bottling*" is used, it signifies that 100% of the wine has been made by the estate.
6. *Type*—Indicates whether the wine is a varietal, generic, or a proprietary brand. A varietal designation, by law, means that it must contain at least 51% of the variety named.

Some vintners list on the back label the varieties of grapes used in addition to a description of the wine.

NEW YORK

The early settlers made wine from the wild grapes they found growing in abundance, but it was so unpalatable that they sent for European varieties of vines, which promptly died in the harsher climate of the New World. Native varieties were cultivated and developed, producing excellent wines having their own distinct flavor and character, quite different from those made in Europe.

Commercial wine making in the New York region began in 1860 at the head of Keuka Lake, around Hammondsport where thirty years earlier the first cultivated wine grapes had been successfully planted. A number of unsuccessful attempts were made to grow European grape varieties over the years, but it was not until quite recently that Dr. Konstantin Frank demonstrated that *Vitis vinifera* could be grown in New York State. Other New York growers have established sizable plantings of French hybrids along with the extensive *Vitis labrusca* plantings traditional to the region.

Most New York wines are extensively blended, producing a consistent uniform quality dictated to a large extent by the consumers. In general, New York sparkling wines are outstanding, closely followed by the varietal whites. A number of red wines are improving year by year, some of them reaching the quality level of the whites.

The rather strong fragrance of the *Vitis labrusca* is often modified by blending, although some vintners continue to produce wines with the full native flavor, called "foxiness" by its critics. The vinifera wines are completely free of that taste, as are the French hybrid wines.

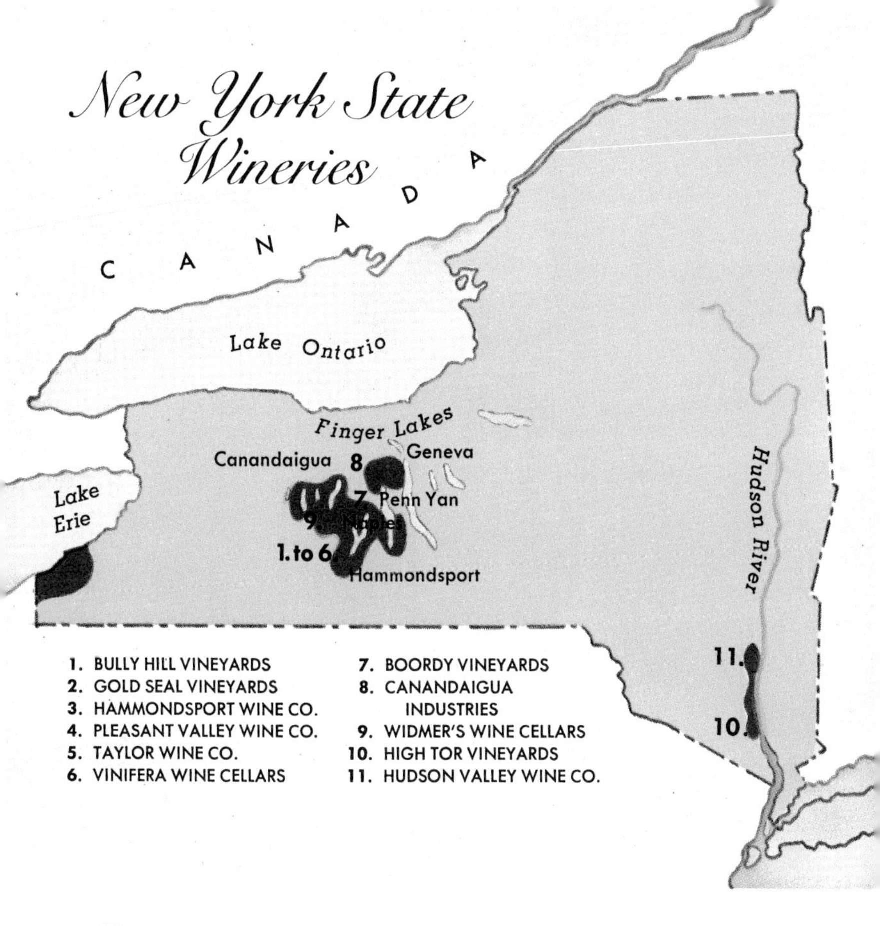

The map shows the principal wine-growing areas of New York State. The largest by far is the Finger Lakes Region where the great majority of wineries are located, particularly along the western shore of Keuka Lake. The other regions include the Hudson River Valley, Chautauqua, and Niagara. The Chautauqua wine-growing belt extends along Lake Erie, through Pennsylvania and winds up in Ohio. The plantings consist mostly of Concord grapes, much used for Kosher wine. Some of the Niagara wine region lies in Canada as well as New York between Lakes Erie and Ontario.

THE FINGER LAKES REGION vineyards and wineries are clustered chiefly around Lakes Keuka and Canandaigua. There are some plantings near Seneca, Cayuga, and Hemlock. The water has a tempering effect on the harsh winter, producing a nearly ideal climate for viticulture. Years ago there were many small wineries here. Today there are less than a dozen.

GOLD SEAL WINERIES, founded in 1865, entered their modern phase of wine making in the 1940's with the arrival of Charles Fournier, a Chief Wine Master from France. He set about improving the wines, selecting native varietals and, with Philip Wagner, planting hybrids suited to the New York climate. Next he enlisted the aid of Dr. Konstantin Frank who, despite three centuries of failures by other vintners, believed and proved that *vinifera* could be grown in New York State. All three approaches were crowned with success.

Gold Seal's top premium wines, marketed under the Charles Fournier signature, include the *Chablis Nature* and the sparkling *Fournier Blanc de Blancs,* both made with Chardonnay grown in the Finger Lakes Region.

A large selection of premium varietals, generics, and champagnes are sold under the Gold Seal label, such as:
Red Table Wines: Catawba Red, Concord Red, and Burgundy.
White Table Wines: Catawba White, Rhine, and Sauterne.
Rosé Table Wines: Catawba Pink, and Rosé.
Sparkling Wines: Gold Seal Brut, Extra Dry, Pink, Sparkling Burgundy, and Cold Duck.

A lower-priced selection of still and sparkling wines is sold under the *Henri Marchant* label.

GREAT WESTERN is the most famous of the wines made by the Pleasant Valley Wine Company, a leader in New York wines since 1860. A winner of many international awards, Great Western received its first Gold Medal in Paris in 1867.

Great Western, like many Eastern vintners, prides itself on the quality and fragrance of its native grape wines. A number of French hybrids have been added, as well as some American hybrids. The vintners use traditional methods carefully coordinated with modern technology.

All Great Western Champagne is fermented in the bottle in the traditional manner.

The Sherries and Ports are blended and aged in soleras started a number of years ago, producing wines of distinct quality and unique flavor.

Red Table Wines: *Varietals*—Chelois, Baco Noir (Burgundy), and Vin Rouge. One *generic* is made, the Pleasant Valley Red.

White Table Wines: *Varietals*—Aurora (Sauterne), Dutchess (Rhine Wine), Delaware, Diamond, and Vin Blanc Sec.

Rosé Table Wines: Isabella Rosé, and Pink Catawba.

Champagnes: Brut, Special Reserve, Extra Dry, and Pink.

BULLY HILL VINEYARDS, on the site of the original Taylor Wine Company, is owned and operated by the highly individualistic Walter S. Taylor, a direct descendant of the famous New York State wine family.

In 1970, only two wines were made using native and French-American varieties. The grapes, grown on the estate and adjoining lands legally claim the Estate-Bottled appellation.

The *Bully Hill White Wine* is a blend of Delaware, Aurora, and Seyval Blanc varieties.

The *Bully Hill Red Wine* is a blend of seven varieties.

To these two original wines a Rosé and six varietals have been added: Delaware, Baco Noir, Ives Noir, Aurora Blanc, Seyval Blanc, and Diamond.

Walter Taylor is justly proud of his wines, closely supervising each step of the process in the vineyard as well as in the winery. A man of many talents, he is proudest of his title of "vigneron."

Vineyards on the slopes of Lake Keuka, one of the Finger Lakes.

THE TAYLOR WINE COMPANY, the largest in the state, and one of the largest in the country, operates its winery in a smoothly meshed combination of traditional wine making methods and the latest technological advances.

Walter Taylor's original seven acres, bought in 1880, have multiplied more than a hundredfold, and several thousand acres of neighboring vineyards help fill the many giant fermenting tanks in the modern winery.

Extensive French hybrid plantings are supplementing and sometimes replacing the native grape. The wine from the hybrids is blended with other wines, creating totally new wines with a variety of flavors never known before.

Like the majority of New York wines, Taylor's are light and fragrant. Through careful blending, the different wines offer a rather wide range of the characteristic *labrusca* fragrance.

In the late '60s Taylor introduced a new wine, Lake Country Red, followed by a Lake Country White and a Pink. Besides the table wines and the justly famous champagnes, Taylor makes a full line of dessert wines and two vermouths.

Red Table Wines: Burgundy, Claret, and Lake Country Red.

White Table Wines: Sauterne, Rhine Wine, and Lake Country White.

Rosé Table Wines: Rosé, and Lake Country Pink.

Sparkling Wines: Dry Champagne, Brut, and Pink. Sparkling Burgundy and Cold Duck.

Appetizer Wines: Pale Dry Cocktail Sherry, Dry and Sweet Vermouths.

Dessert Wines: Port, Tawny Port, Sherry, Cream Sherry, White Tokay, and Muscatel.

WIDMER'S WINE CELLARS were founded in 1882 by John Jacob Widmer in the hills of Naples, at the foot of Lake Canandaigua. His son Will made the wine.

The Widmer philosophy was that the white wines made from the native grape were unique and, carefully vinified, would be the match of any other wines.

The Widmers enlisted the aid of Phil Wagner and other hybridizers and were among the pioneers of fine hybrid stocks in the East.

Among the large choice of wines and champagnes are:

Varietal Whites: Delaware, Riesling, Moore's Diamond, Vergennes, and Elvira.

VINIFERA WINE CELLARS and vineyards are the home of Dr. Konstantin Frank, the passionate apostle of *Vitis vinifera* in the East. Dr. Frank's German parents had established vineyards in the Ukraine where he developed his considerable skills, bringing them to the Finger Lakes in the '40s. There he was befriended by that other great wine maker, Charles Fournier, and was able to prove his contention that *vinifera* could be grown in the Northeast, using the three hundred years of previous failures as an example of what should not be done.

Dr. Frank's sixty acres are all planted in European vines, all of them thriving.

He has made all kinds of wines from these grapes, some for marketing, some just to prove his point, such as the Johannisberg Trockenbeeren Auslese which sold for forty-five dollars a bottle!

Although his wines are on the market, primarily the Johannisberg Riesling Natur Spätlese, Pinot Chardonnay Natur, and Gewürztraminer, his operation cannot be considered a true commercial enterprise. He is always demonstrating, for the benefit of the vintners who will follow him, the superlative excellence of vinifera wines and the demand they create among discriminating consumers.

He has also produced Cabernet Sauvignon, Pinot Gris from the only commercial planting of this Alsatian grape, Pinot Noir, a sweet wine from the Russian grape Sereksia, Gamay Beaujolais, and Aligoté. The last is a Burgundian grape producing a light, fresh wine with a pleasant tartness. The mere existence of these varieties in New York State caused amazement in the 1960's, and the next step for their maker was to make the public realize their excellence.

Dr. Konstantin Frank examining his Riesling grapes after the first frost, in Hammondsport.

THE HUDSON RIVER VALLEY'S wineries of note are on the majestic river's western banks, from the Tappan Zee opposite Tarrytown north to Highland. All are relatively small, but each has its dreams and plans of expansion to meet the ever-increasing demand for fine New York State wines.

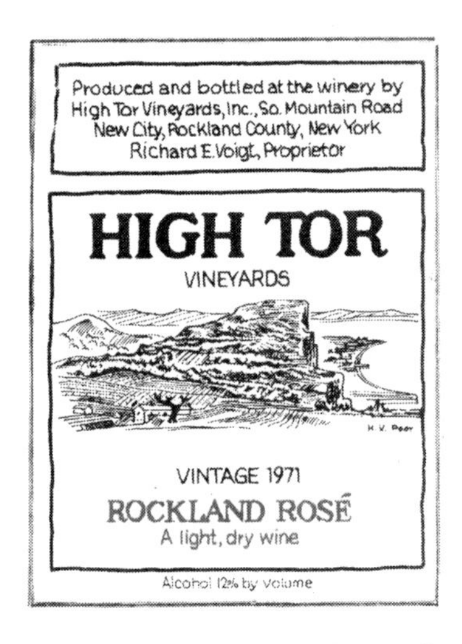

HIGH TOR VINEYARDS, on the southern slopes of the mountain immortalized by Maxwell Anderson and from which it takes its name, is considered by many to be the best vineyard of the district. It was founded by Everett Crosby, a writer turned vintner, and sold in the 1970's to Richard Voigt who plans to expand and continue the fine wine making tradition established by Crosby.

The vineyard is planted in native grapes and hybrids from the Wagner nurseries and only three wines, a red, a white, and a rosé are produced in modest quantities.

Crosby had named his wines, in proud simplicity, Rockland Red, Rockland White, and Rockland Rosé. A special selection made in outstanding vintage years bears the notation, "Special Reserve," and the year.

THE HUDSON VALLEY WINE COMPANY is located on a bluff overlooking the river. It was founded in 1907 by the Bolognesi family. The grapes grown are the native varieties with a predominance of Delaware and Catawba. The wines are estate-bottled.

Table Wines: Pink Catawba, Pink Chablis, Burgundy, Chablis, Haut Sauterne and Sauterne.

Sparkling Wines: Blanc de Blancs Champagne, Brut, Extra Dry, and Pink Champagne. There is also a Sparkling Burgundy and Cold Duck.

BENMARL VINEYARDS is an unusual organization, a small co-operative grape-growing association formed to produce fine wines for its members, *The Benmarl Societé des Vignerons.*

The Societé, whose members are mostly business, academic and professional people maintain a model vineyard estate and winery. The vines are French-American and *vinifera* varieties. Membership is by purchase of "Vinerights," each Vineright representing two actual grapevines, producing one case of wine each vintage year for its owner.

THE CHAUTAUQUA AND NIAGARA REGIONS may prove to be the next area of expansion for French hybrids in New York State. It has been traditionally planted in Concord and other American varieties, but plantings of hybrids may totally change this region.

BOORDY VINEYARDS made a big jump from Riderwood, Maryland to Penn Yan, N.Y., and the Yakima Valley in Washington. Production is supervised by Jocelyn and Philip Wagner, who founded the original Boordy Vineyard in 1943.

The first vintage was a *Red Wine,* resembling French Beaujolais and a fragrant white called Boordyblümchen, soon followed by a dry *White Wine,* and a *Rosé Wine.* In the early '70s a number of varietals and proprietary wines were added.

OTHER STATES also produce wines, but in much smaller quantities than New York and California. There are the Boordy Vineyard of Maryland, Meier's Wine Cellars of Ohio, a cluster of wineries around Erie, Pennsylvania, The American Wine Company of Missouri, and Wiederkehr of Arkansas, to name a few.

There is promise in experimental plantings of wine grapes in fruit-growing areas of Oregon, Washington, Georgia, and Illinois. The research of the various agricultural stations such as Davis, California, and Geneva, New York, combined with the pioneering work of Charles Fournier, Dr. Konstantin Frank, Maynard Amerine, and V.L. Singleton provide a store of knowledge for a bright future for American wines.

FRANCE

For centuries French wines have enjoyed and deserved the reputation of being the best in the world. The great French wines are still unmatched and unexcelled. While the lesser French wines are being challenged, with more or less success, they still hold their prominent position in the marketplace.

Ideal climate and soil conditions for viticulture give French wines a great and unchanging advantage. The selection of the grape variety best suited for the particular location, arrived at through centuries of trial and error, is another plus. Scientific advances in agronomy and viticulture are helping to close the gap on this advantage in other countries. Finally there is the superb skill of the French vintners, passed from father to son through generations along with an almost mystical sixth sense of relationship that the "vigneron" has with his grapes. All these combine to produce the wines which have delighted generations of wine lovers all over the world.

All French grapes are of the *Vitis vinifera* group. The so-called "noble" grapes, such as the Pinots and the Cabernets, produce the great wines. Lesser strains, such as the Gamay, produce wines of excellent quality and the great volume of the good, honest *vin ordinaire* which graces most French tables.

All wine-producing countries make some inferior wine. The French are not immune from this defect. Because they produce so much wine, there is always a sizable quantity of mediocre to out-and-out poor wine which is foisted on both the French and export markets by unscrupulous wine merchants or poorly trained wine buyers for export firms.

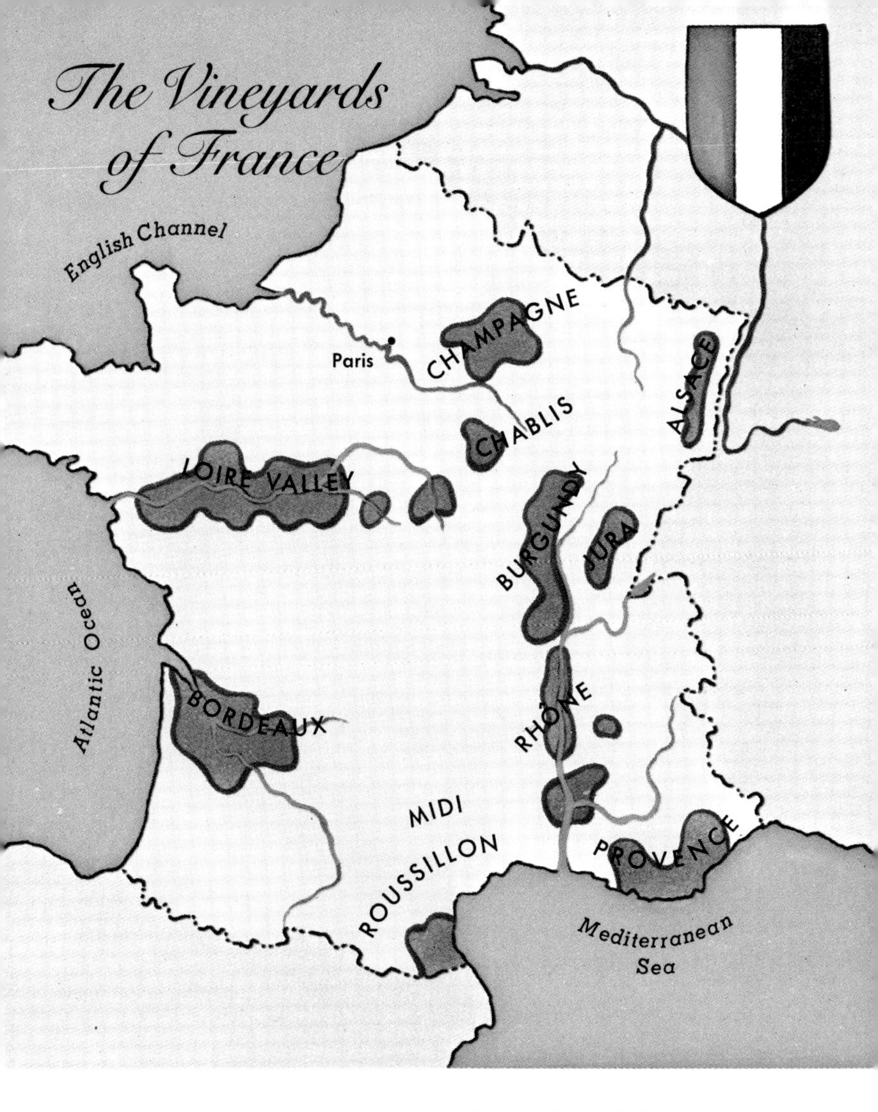

Wine grapes are grown over most of France by individual growers for their own needs. Only the major areas, producing wine for commercial purposes are shown on this map. The wine regions are strictly limited by law, as are the names of the wines grown in any area. The geographic extent of a wine-producing area is not necessarily an indication of its importance, the amount of wine it produces, or the relative excellence of the wine. More detailed maps are found on the pages following.

BORDEAUX

The wines of Bordeaux date back twenty centuries, to the time of Imperial Rome. In 1152, Eleanor of Aquitaine married Henry II of England and for three hundred years Bordeaux was under English domination. The English grew fond of the wine they named *claret,* establishing a major market for it to this day.

The Bordeaux Region is actually the 2.5 million-acre French Department of the Gironde. Its vineyards cover about 300,000 acres, producing about half of the quality wine of France in its 39 individually recognized districts. The map shows some major districts.

The wines range across a very broad spectrum of taste, from the elegant and delicate Médoc reds to the rich and suave Château d'Yquem, the king of the Sauternes.

In 1855, an official classification of the greatest châteaux wines of the Médoc, Sauternes, and Barsac districts was drawn up. In the 1950's those of Graves and St. Émilion were added. There has been a widespread feeling that the classification should be revised and include most of the other districts. Of the more than 2,000 châteaux of Bordeaux some 200 have been classified at one time or another. The classification has some use for the consumer, but it is no longer an accurate yardstick for comparison.

The whole region is completely wine-centered. Wine fraternities abound and provide more than a touch of color with their medieval costumes at festive occasions. Most date back to the Middle Ages, such as the Jurade of St. Émilion, which received its charter from John Lackland, King of England, in 1199. All are united under the Grand Conseil de Bordeaux.

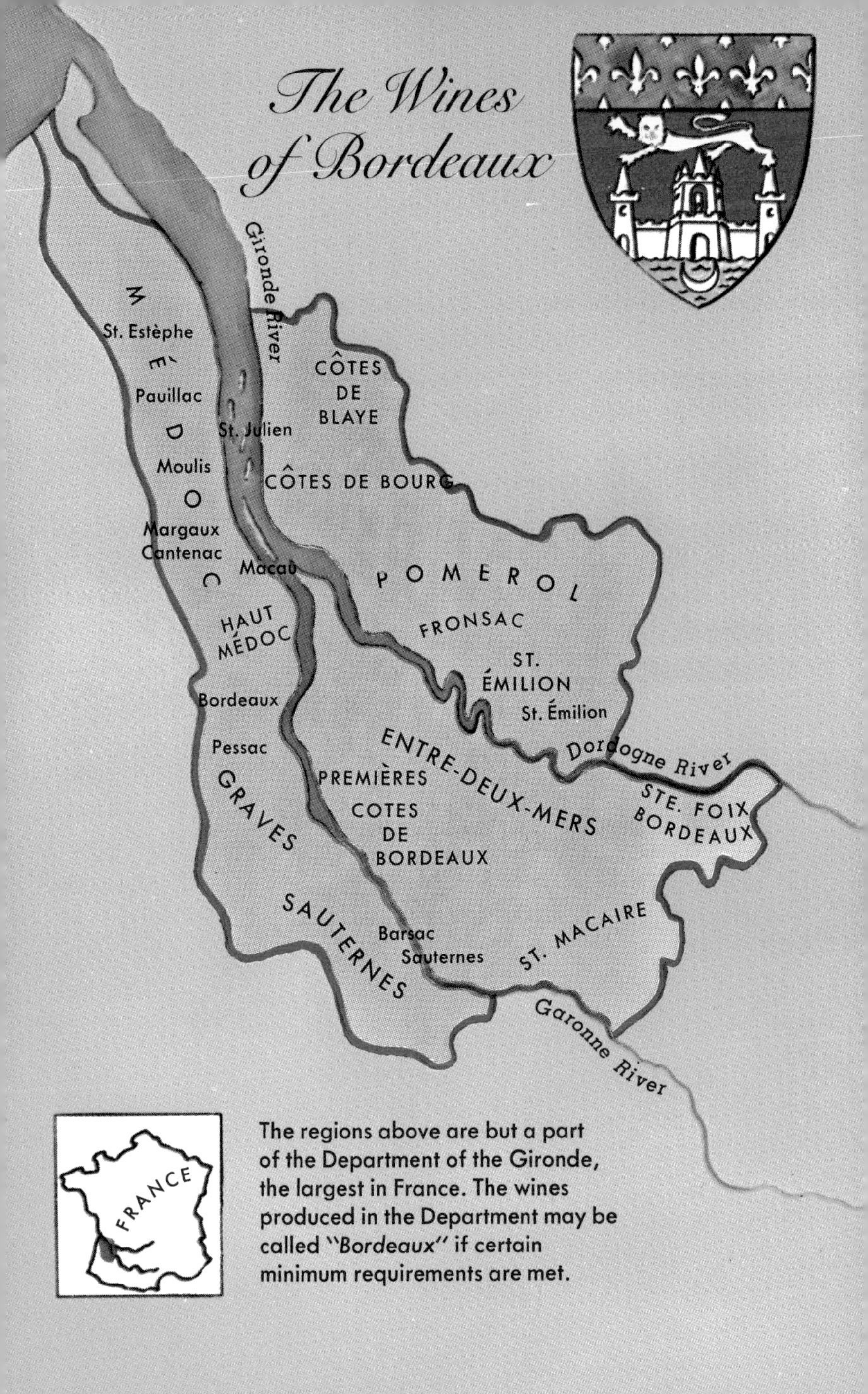
The Wines of Bordeaux
Gironde River
MÉDOC
St. Estèphe
Pauillac
St. Julien
Moulis
Margaux
Cantenac
Macau
CÔTES DE BLAYE
CÔTES DE BOURG
POMEROL
HAUT MÉDOC
FRONSAC
ST. ÉMILION
St. Émilion
Bordeaux
Pessac
GRAVES
PREMIÈRES COTES DE BORDEAUX
ENTRE-DEUX-MERS
Dordogne River
STE. FOIX BORDEAUX
SAUTERNES
Barsac
Sauternes
ST. MACAIRE
Garonne River
FRANCE
The regions above are but a part of the Department of the Gironde, the largest in France. The wines produced in the Department may be called "Bordeaux" if certain minimum requirements are met.

THE FIRST GREAT GROWTHS of Bordeaux, eight reds and one white, are considered by many connoisseurs to be the greatest wines in the world and the peers of the *Grand Crus* of Burgundy. These wines take several years to develop. They are usually aged from two to three years in the cask and an additional five years or so in the bottle. In the great vintage years they may need a decade to reach their peak, and will then hold it, continuing to develop more subtle nuances for another ten years or more. These wines are rare, much sought after, and as a result, quite costly.

These great châteaux wines are listed with their district, commune, and the average yearly production in cases (at 12 bottles to a case).

Haut-Brion	*Graves, Pessac*	10,000 cases
Lafite-Rothschild	*Médoc, Pauillac*	15,000 cases
Latour	*Médoc, Pauillac*	16,000 cases
Mouton-Rothschild	*Médoc, Pauillac*	11,000 cases
Margaux	*Médoc, Margaux*	12,000 cases
Cheval-Blanc	*St. Émilion*	12,000 cases
Ausone	*St. Émilion*	3,000 cases
Pétrus	*Pomerol*	2,500 cases
d'Yquem	*Sauternes*	9,000 cases

Like a fairy-tale castle, the battlements and ivy-covered towers of the Château d'Yquem rise above the plain, dominating the countryside as its extraordinary wine dominates the Sauternes district. Thomas Jefferson, a great wine connoisseur of his time, praised it as "the best white wine of France." It is the only Bordeaux white awarded the classification of a First Great Growth.

THE MÉDOC, a narrow triangle of land extending northward from the city of Bordeaux, is considered the greatest wine district in the world. It produces more wines of high quality than any other, the best of them from the southern portion called "Haut Médoc." The wines are sometimes labeled *Haut-Médoc,* more often under the name of the communes of *Margaux, St. Julien, Pauillac,* or *St. Estèphe,* and most often under the name of the château.

The Château Pichon-Longueville, an example of beautiful architecture of the Médoc district.

Margaux wines are big and full, need several years to mature and are superior companions to meat dishes and turkey. Some of its best châteaux:

Brane-Cantenac
Cantemerle
Chasse-Spleen
Giscours
Lascombes
Palmer
Rausan-Ségla
Prieuré-Lichine
Kirwan
Boyd-Cantenac
Marquis-de-Terme
Villegeorge

Pauillac wines are long-lived and renowned for their balance. Along with the three First Great Growths of this commune are these outstanding châteaux:

Duhart-Milon
Lynch-Bages
Pichon-Longueville
Pontet-Canet
Haut-Batailley
Haut-Bagès-Libéral
Calvé-Croizet-Bagès
Pédesclaux
La Couronne
Batailley
Grand-Puy-Lacoste
Clerc-Milon-Mondon

Saint-Julien wines are light, delicate, relatively short-lived. Some of the best:

Beychevelle
Branaire-Ducru
Ducru-Beaucaillou
Langoa-Barton
Léoville-Barton
LaTour-Carnet
Léoville-Poyferré
Belgrave
Moulin-Riche

Saint-Estèphe wines are considered the fullest wines of the Médoc. Some of its outstanding châteaux are:

Calon-Ségur
Cos d'Estournel
Cos-Labory
Phélan-Ségur
Montrose
Ormes-de-Pez
De Pez
Rochet

THE SAINT-ÉMILION wines were not classified until 1955, although its wines were famous as far back as the 4th century. It is planted with over 16,000 acres of vines and today produces more high quality wines than any other division. The wines are sturdy, generous, and many are pleasant when young. The great châteaux bottlings of this division are the equals of the Médocs.

The Premiers Grands Crus of St. Émilion include:

Beauséjour-Fagouet
Belair
Canon
Figeac
Pavie
Cheval-Blanc
Ausone
Clos Fourtet

In addition to the dozen First Great Growths produced from its vineyards, St. Émilion has some sixty-odd Great Growths, and almost a thousand wines which are classified as Principal and Lesser Growths.

ENTRE-DEUX-MERS is one of the major divisions of Bordeaux. Its name, meaning "between two seas" is a slight misnomer, as it is located between two rivers, the Garonne and the Dordogne. It produces a vast amount of white wine, almost ten million gallons in a good year, which is inexpensive and of good everyday quality. The red wines of this division are sold as *Bordeaux* or as *Bordeaux Supérieur.*

POMEROL wines are not yet officially classified. Château Pétrus is recognized as the Great Growth of the region with the following châteaux rated close behind:

Beauregard
Certan-Giraud
Certan-de-May
Gazin
La Conseillante
La Croix
Lafleur-Pétrus
Lagrange
Vieux-Château-Certan
Latour-Pomerol
l'Église Clinet
l'Évangile
Petit-Village
Nénin
Rouget
Trotanoy
La Pointe

There are some two hundred principal growths of the Pomerol region in addition to those listed above. These wines are given the appelations *Pomerol* and *Lalande de Pomerol.*

SAUTERNES AND BARSAC produce the sweet rich golden white wines of Bordeaux. By definition there is no French "Dry Sauternes." The average production of the district is about 300,000 cases a year. The Sauternes and Barsac district is a strictly delimited area consisting of the following five townships: Preignac, Bommes, Fargues, Barsac, and Sauternes.

The vineyards were classified in 1855 with the great Château d'Yquem classed as the only First Great Growth. Eleven

First Growths are listed, and twelve Second Growths. Some of the best known are these châteaux:

La Tour-Blanche
Lafaurie-Peyraguey
Rabaud-Sigalas
Climens
Arche
Filhot
Suau

Over three hundred Minor Growths are also listed, some as *Château,* some as *Crus,* and some as *Clos,* while a few are listed as *Domaines.*

FRONSAC is a relatively small district of Bordeaux producing about 400,000 gallons of robust wine similar, but of slightly less finesse than the Pomerols. The best bear the appellation *Côtes-Canon-Fronsac,* and a slightly lower grade carry *Côtes-de-Fronsac* on the label. The combined total produced from this district is slightly over one hundred Principal Growths. These wines have not yet been officially classified.

GRAVES is one of the larger districts of Bordeaux, producing an average of two million gallons a year. About one quarter of this amount is red wine, the rest is white. The Château Haut-Brion, the greatest among the red wines produced in the district, was classified in 1855 with the Médocs, and all the other wines were ignored until they were at last classified in 1953 and 1959.

There are thirteen classified red wines of Graves, including Haut-Brion. Some of the better known châteaux of the district are listed below:

Bouscault
Carbonnieux
Domaine de Chevalier
La Mission-Haut-Brion
Smith-Haut-Lafitte
La Tour-Haut-Brion
Olivier
Pape-Clément
Haut-Bailly

There are eight classified white wines of Graves:

Bouscault
Carbonnieux
Domaine de Chevalier
Couhins
La Tour-Martillac
Laville-Haut-Brion
Malartic-Lagravière
Olivier

There are over four hundred other Principal Growths in the Graves district. Some of these produce only red wine, some produce only white, while a large number produce both red and white wine.

THE CÔTES DE BLAYE is the remaining large district of Bordeaux, located on the right bank of the Gironde estuary, opposite the Médoc. It produces about four million gallons of average to mediocre quality wine, mostly white. The best grades, either red or white are sold as *Premières Côtes de Blaye.* The others are usually labeled *Bordeaux Blanc,* and *Bordeaux Rouge.* In most years the red is better than the white.

BURGUNDY

For more than 2,000 years the Burgundians have tended their vines, proud in the knowledge that their wines are among the very greatest in the world. The region is not large, and the amount of wine made is relatively small. It amounts to less than 2% of the total French production.

Almost half of the wine produced is Beaujolais. A third is good honest wine of no great distinction. The remaining one-fifth, or a little more than five million gallons, is the total production of all the great wines such as the Chablis, Chambertins, Cortons, Montrachets, Meursaults, Pommards, etc., sought by gourmets all over the world.

The two principal grapes producing the great wines are Pinot Noir and Chardonnay, both having a very low yield of wine per acre. The Gamay is the grape of Beaujolais. This grape is a more generous bearer, but it is planted almost exclusively in the Beaujolais region.

The character of Burgundian wines, whether red or white, varies from one vineyard to another. Each wine is a true individual, being quite distinct from its neighbor. While this distinctiveness offers the wine lover a wide spectrum of taste, it does not permit much scope in the way of generalizations about the characteristics of the wines.

The great red Burgundies have an unsurpassed combination of fullness and finesse with characteristics of warmth, bouquet, fruitiness and flavor all present in exquisite balance. The great white Burgundies are dry, clean and fresh tasting. They are also remarkably full and beautifully balanced. Burgundies have been favorites of gourmets for years and years.

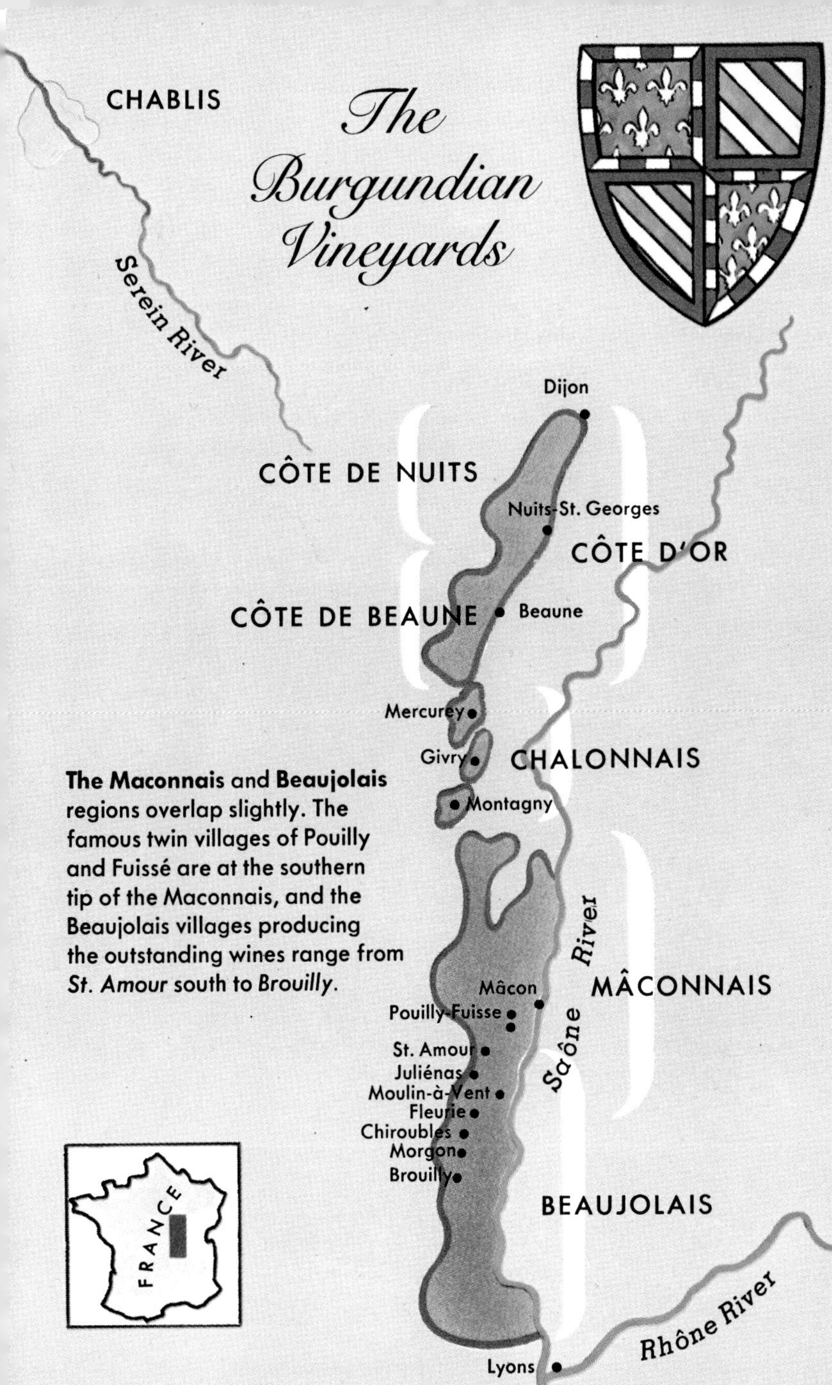

The Burgundian Vineyards
CHABLIS
Serein River
Dijon
CÔTE DE NUITS
Nuits-St. Georges
CÔTE D'OR
CÔTE DE BEAUNE
Beaune
Mercurey
Givry
CHALONNAIS
Montagny
The Maconnais and **Beaujolais** regions overlap slightly. The famous twin villages of Pouilly and Fuissé are at the southern tip of the Maconnais, and the Beaujolais villages producing the outstanding wines range from *St. Amour* south to *Brouilly*.
Saône River
Mâcon
MÂCONNAIS
Pouilly-Fuisse
St. Amour
Juliénas
Moulin-à-Vent
Fleurie
Chiroubles
Morgon
Brouilly
FRANCE
BEAUJOLAIS
Rhône River
Lyons

BURGUNDY is divided into five major wine-growing areas: *Chablis,* separated from the long narrow strip of the Côte d'Or, some seventy miles northwest of Dijon; the Côte *de Nuits,* the home of the great Chambertin, Vougeot, and Vosne-Romanée; the Côte *de Beaune,* with its share of great names; the tiny Côte *Chalonnaise,* and further south its large neighbor, the *Mâconnais.* At the southernmost point lies the region of the ever-popular and abundant *Beaujolais.*

CHABLIS is a wine name appropriated by every wine-producing country in the world for every possible type of white, and even pink, wine. True Chablis is one of the world's most distinctive wines. Its taste defies description and is so unusual that some who like the imitations may find the real thing too much for them.

Grand Cru Chablis is a long-lasting, strong wine. It has a greenish cast when young, becoming golden-green with age. It comes from only seven small vineyards: *Bougros, Les Preuses, Vaudésir, Grenouilles, Valmur, Les Clos,* and *Blanchot.*

Premiers Crus are a little less intense than the Grands Crus, slightly less alcoholic, and correspondingly less impressive in flavor and aroma. Some of the best are: *Montée de Tonnerre, Côte de Léchet, Monts de Milieu, Fourchaume, Vaillons, Beauroy, Vaucoupin, Vosgros,* and *Les Fourneaux.*

Somewhat lesser wines bear the *Chablis* appellation without a vineyard name. These are very good wines but a step down in character and strength from the Premiers Crus.

Finally there is the *Petit Chablis* produced in the outskirts of the area. It is pleasant but undistinguished, often acid, and weaker in flavor and strength.

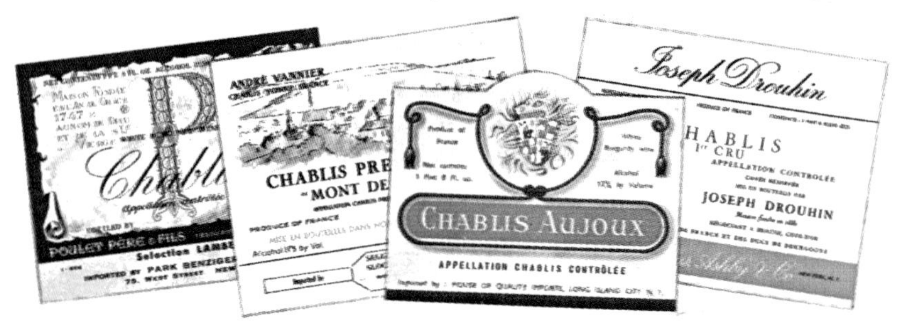

THE CÔTE DE NUITS, ranging from Fixin in the north to Prémeaux in the south, has some of the world's greatest red wines. The finesse and velvety warmth of its Grands Crus are considered utimate perfection by many gourmets. Very little white wine is made but it shares the quality of the prestigious reds.

The Grands Crus of the Côte de Nuits include: *Le Chambertin, Chambertin-Clos de Bèze, Charmes-Chambertin,* and six others bearing the name of the vineyard followed by the magic name of Chambertin; *Clos de Tart; Les Bonnes Mares; Clos de la Roche; St. Denis; Les Musigny; Les Petits Musigny; Clos de Vougeot; Les Echézaux; Les Grands Echézaux; La Tâche; Le Richebourg; La Romanée-Conti; La Romanée;* and *Romanée-St. Vivant.*

Premiers Crus abound on this northern end of the Golden Slope and many of them come very close to the quality of their neighboring Grands Crus. The wines of *Fixin* deserve to be better known. They bear a strong resemblance to their more famous neighbor, *Gevrey-Chambertin.* In the latter township there are about a dozen Premier Cru vineyards. *Morey-St. Denis* has about twice as many. In *Chambolle-Musigny* there are two vineyards whose names are expressive of the wines produced, *Les Charmes* and *Les Amoureuses.* A score of other vineyards, less poetically named, also produce wines of great charm and distinction. So much of *Vougeot* and *Vosne-Romanée* is taken up by Grands Crus that one can tend to forget the superb wines of surrounding vineyards. The wines of *Prémeaux* are marketed under the name of the larger commune of *Nuits-St. Georges.* The wines are big and of very high and consistent quality. At their best they bear a strong resemblance to the Chambertins.

THE CÔTE DE BEAUNE produces, in addition to the superb reds typical of the Côte d'Or, the great Burgundian whites of Corton and Montrachet. From the dull little spa of Santenay, whose good but rather undistinguished wines are overshadowed by the spectacular ones to the north, to the tiny village of Pernand-Vergelesses, Premier Cru vineyards crowd the slopes.

The Grands Crus begin at Aloxe-Corton with the great vineyards of *Corton-Charlemagne: Le Corton; Les Chaumes; Le Clos du Roi; Les Perrières; Les Renardes; Les Meix; Les Bressandes,* and several others. In Puligny-Montrachet we find: *Le Montrachet; Chevalier-Montrachet;* and *Bâtard-Montrachet.*

Premiers Crus are everywhere, the best usually alongside the Grands Crus vineyards. Many of these wines are sold at the annual Hospices de Beaune auction that is a tradition of the region. Both reds and whites are forceful, memorable wines, and classed among the best in Burgundy.

THE CHALONNAIS and THE MÂCONNAIS are the smallest and largest slopes, respectively, in Burgundy. As the demand for Burgundy wine has increased, the wines of these two less distinguished regions have helped fill the need. The best of the Chalonnais, the red *Mercurey* and the white *Montagny,* have won merited approval. The plain, honest wines of Mâcon have also come into their own. At the southern end of the Mâconnais is the remarkable district of *Pouilly-Fuissé* and its Chardonnay white wines.

THE BEAUJOLAIS REGION, much hillier than the Côte d'Or, is the southernmost part of Burgundy. Its granitic and clayey soil works a subtle miracle on the Gamay grape, which is virtually outlawed in the rest of Burgundy. The result is the delightful, fruity, light wine so popular everywhere. It is now the fashion to drink the wine very young, but many connoisseurs consider that the better Beaujolais are at their peak with some aging, in the bottle as well as in the barrel.

THE BEST BEAUJOLAIS are those bearing the names of the following nine villages: *Brouilly; Côte-de-Brouilly; Chénas; Chiroubles; Fleurie; Juliénas; Moulin-à-Vent; Morgon;* and *St. Amour*. In good years these will have distinct characteristics setting them apart from the oceans of more ordinary Beaujolais. There are 26 other villages producing better-than-average quality wine, and these are classified as *Beaujolais-Villages,* entitled to that appellation on the label.

Fleurie and Chiroubles are the most luscious and the lightest.
Morgon is longest lived.
Juliénas has body and vigor.
Moulin-à-Vent, considered by many the "best" Beaujolais, is a dark, strong wine, and has a reputation for very good keeping qualities.
St. Amour is light and fragrant.
Brouilly and **Côte-de-Brouilly** are grapey and rich.
Chénas is the strongest.
Beaujolais Supérieur is a good grade of wine with a bit more alcoholic content than the ordinary variety, 10% as against 9%, minimum.

Good ordinary Beaujolais is a very pleasant wine, all too easy to gulp down. It makes up a large portion of the 15 million gallons produced yearly.

ALSACE

The fine wines of Alsace, the ancient border province of France, deserve to be better known. The climate and soil are very similar to those of the neighboring Rhine valley vineyards, and even the grape varieties are the same, with a few exceptions. While the German vintner tries for sweetness, the Alsatian looks for strength and body. He may be making a "Germanic" wine, but he makes it the French way. His is a wine to accompany the superb and savory cuisine of Alsace, one of France's great gastronomic regions.

Unlike those of other wine regions of France, the wines are usually named after the variety of grape used. The place-name is secondary.

THE VINEYARDS stretch along a narrow strip, running almost due north-south for 70-odd miles. The small central portion, between Guebviller and Ribeauvillé, produces the finest wines. Almost all Alsatian wine is white; plus some *rosé* and *gris*.

THE CHIEF VARIETIES of grapes are: *Riesling; Gewürztraminer; Pinot Gris,* or *Tokay d'Alsace; Sylvaner; Muscat d'Alsace;* and *Pinot Blanc.*

THE FAMOUS WINE TOWNS, often on the label following the varietal name, are: Riquewihr, Bergheim, Ammerschwihr, Ribeauvillé, Kaysersberg, and Guebwiller.

The Alsatian Riesling is a dry, fresh-tasting, fruity wine capable of great finesse.

Gewürztraminer, a very spicy white, is strong in bouquet and taste. It is, with Chablis, one of the two most individual-tasting French white wines.

Sylvaner, best when young, is a light, fresh white wine.

Tokay D'Alsace, no relation to Hungarian Tokay, is a full-bodied dry or slightly sweet wine.

Pinot Blanc resembles the Sylvaner, but has more body.

Zwicker is a blend of great and common varieties.

Edelzwicker is a blend of great or "noble" varieties only.

PROVENCE

The wines of Provence reflect the character of this region of gaiety and sunshine, the land of the troubadours and the Courts of Love. With its sun-drenched slopes facing the Mediterranean, Provence stretches from Marseille to Nice. About 150 million gallons of wine are made in this region every year. Much of the wine is rosé, rated among the best in France. The reds bear some resemblance to Italian wines, and are lively and heady. The whites have a quality described as "tarpaulin edged with lace."

A profusion of grape varieties are used in making Provençal wines. The most practical indication of quality is the place-name.

BANDOL, a small fishing village, lends its name to an area of about 300 acres of vineyards producing some 100,000 gallons of mostly red and rosé, with some white. They are typically pleasant and vigorous.

CASSIS, another little seaport, halfway between Bandol and Marseille, makes the most renowned rosé and white, the ideal companions for the *bouillabaisse* of Marseille.

BELLET, just a few miles northeast of Nice, grows its wines in a flinty soil which imparts a delightful taste to the reds, rosés and whites made there.

PALETTE, near Aix-en-Provence, also produces red, rosé, and white wines. The whites are among the best in the region.

CÔTES DE PROVENCE is the legal appellation of slightly lesser wines than the four above, although they are very pleasant and of good quality. If they meet the proper standards they bear the V.D.Q.S. official stamp. The letters stand for *Vins Délimités de Qualité Supérieure,* or "Delimited Wines of Superior Quality." This classification is not lightly given and is a reasonable guarantee of a secondary range of the better wines.

THE RHÔNE VALLEY

The fast-flowing Rhône, as it cut its valley from Vienne to Avignon, created the site of some of the finest vineyards in southern France. The vineyards fall into a northern and a southern group. In the north, fruit trees are interspersed with the vines; in the south, olive trees add a touch of silver to the riotous vine colors.

The Rhône wines are made from a great number of grape varieties; Châteauneuf-du-Pape is a blend of thirteen! The great reds can reach velvety smoothness and great depth of flavor, the whites can be exquisitely delicate and yet heady.

Too often Rhône wines are not kept long enough to reach their full maturity, which often takes a full decade. They are generally cheaper than other great French wines and are often a bargain by comparison.

CÔTE RÔTIE means "roasted slope," and its grapes, *Syrah* and *Viognier,* sun themselves on the steep terraces. Its two parts, the Côte Brune and the Côte Blonde, were named after the brunette and the blonde daughters of the original owner. The slopes, legend has it, took on the characteristics of their comely namesakes.

The wine is red, though a little white *Viognier* is added to the *Syrah* to add finesse.

Château Grillet, rated among the best of the Rhône Valley's white wines, is the smallest French vineyard having its own *Appellation Controlée*. It is dry, full, and well balanced. The grape used is the *Viognier*.

CONDRIEU'S heavily perfumed white wines, long practically unknown outside the district, are becoming famous, and their distinctive taste, due to the granitic soil, makes them acclaimed by connoisseurs. The *Viognier* grape is used to make this delicious wine, which can be fairly dry or moderately sweet depending on the vintage and the vintner.

HERMITAGE wines, both red and white, develop a soft and velvety bigness with aging. The red wine grape is the *Syrah,* the white, mostly *Marsanne.*

The red forms a heavy sediment in aging, and should be decanted. The white is one of the longest-lived dry whites.

The vineyards are among the oldest in France. St. Patrick is reputed to have planted vines there when he came to Gaul.

CHÂTEAUNEUF-DU-PAPE is one of the Côtes du Rhône's finest red wines. A little white wine is also made, very distinctive and pleasant but relatively unknown.

Unlike other Rhône wines, Châteauneuf-du-Pape is a blend of 13 grape varieties. It varies therefore from grower to grower, each having his own formula for his blend, within the most stringent regulations in France. Some of the outstanding vineyards of Châteauneuf-du-Pape are: The Domaines of *Fines Roches, de la Nerthe, de Nalys, de Saint-Préfert,* and *des Sénéchaux;* the *Clos-Saint-Jean; Château de Vaudieu; Château Fortia; La Gardine;* and *Clos-des-Papes.*

SAINT-PÉRAY is renowned for its sparkling wines, much in demand by the French who thriftily substitute them for Champagne. The still white wines have considerable body and bouquet.

TAVEL makes rosés exclusively. The *Grenache* grape is the major constituent, and there is little variation in vintage years. Tavel is the world's best-known rosé wine. *Château d'Aqueria* is probably the best Tavel exported. Tavels should not be aged; they are at their best between one and five years old. Shown above is a typical label for a Tavel rosé prepared for export to a wine merchant in the United States. Note designation: *Appellation Controlée.*

OTHER CÔTES DU RHÔNE wines of interest and distinction are those of *Cairanne; Rasteau; Gigondas;* of *Vaqueyras,* and of *Beaumes-de-Venise.* These are all place-names subject to the *Appellation Controlée.* The wines vary a good deal; most are rosés, the others reds and whites.

CHAMPAGNE

The most famous wines in the world, and the only ones with a legal right, under French law, to the name *Champagne,* are grown on some 37,000 acres in a strictly delimited area of the old French province of Champagne. Still wines are also made but are not exported.

The unique quality of the wines is due in great part to climate, the chalky soil, and the skill of the vintners. Most Champagne is a blend of red and white varieties, mostly *Pinot Noir* and *Pinot Chardonnay.*

Besides those simply labeled *Champagne,* there are *Blancs de Noirs,* or white wines made from black grapes, and *Blancs de Blancs,* made from white grapes. Most are made in the *caves* of the big firms cut into the chalk substrata under the cities of Reims and Épernay.

Vineyard or district names are of much less importance than the brand name as an indication of quality. Vintage Champagnes must be tasted and approved by an official committee of experts before they are shipped. No vintage wine may be shipped before it is three years old.

Some of the principal Champagne shippers are: *Ayala-Montebello-Duminy; Bollinger; Charles Heidsieck; De Castellane; Heidsieck-Monopole; Henriot; Irroy; Krug; Lanson; Mercier; Moët et Chandon; Mumm; Perrier-Jouet; Pol Roger; Roederer; Taittinger; Veuve Clicquot;* and *Veuve Laurent-Perrier.*

Champagne is sold in a great variety of bottle sizes:

SIZE	NAME
6.4 oz.	Split
12.8 oz.	Tenth
16 oz.	Pint
26 oz.	Quart
2 qts.	Magnum
4 qts.	Jeroboam
6 qts.	Rehoboam
8 qts.	Methuselah
12 qts.	Salmanasar
16 qts.	Balthazar
20 qts.	Nebuchadnezzar

THE LOIRE AND OTHER REGIONS

Along the banks of the beautiful Loire River, dotted with the most picturesque châteaux of France, are the vineyards of Vouvray, Anjou, and Muscadet. The wines are collectively known as *Vins de la Loire*. All types of table wines, reds, whites, and rosés, are made there, but the best are the still whites. Large amounts of sparkling and semi-sparkling whites, such as the popular *Vouvray,* are also produced.

More than a dozen grape varieties are planted, some exclusively in particular districts. The principal varieties are: *Chenin Blanc,* or *Pineau de la Loire; Cabernet Franc; Chasselas; Muscadet;* and *Sauvignon Blanc*. The varietal names seldom appear on the label.

THE MAJOR DISTRICTS are:

ANJOU. Red, rosé and white wines are made there, with the sweet whites definitely the best.

MUSCADET. The dry white wine bearing the district's name is fast gaining popularity.

TOURAINE. Reds, whites, and rosés are made. The whites are sweet or dry. Home of the famed *Vouvray*.

QUINCY. The dry white wine with a very distinctive clean taste merits wider recognition.

POUILLY-SUR-LOIRE is the home of *Pouilly-Fumé,* a dry white wine resembling the *Quincy*.

OTHER REGIONS and places worth noting include:

ROUSSILLON, bordering on Spain, is a major producer of *vin ordinaire,* and three-quarters of French fortified wines.

JURA, between Burgundy and Switzerland, has great diversity in wines, but not great quality.

SEYSSEL, a small town in the upper Rhône Valley, produces sparkling wine of fine quality.

Chambord, one of the splendid châteaux in the Loire Valley.

GERMANY

All the German wines of distinction are white. They are generally light and fragrant, ranging from 9 to 12 percent in alcohol. The vineyards along the Rhine, Mosel, and Main rivers are near the northernmost limits of the climate belt for grape growing. Often located on steep slopes to catch every ray of the northern sunlight, they are picturesque but physically exhausting to cultivate. The great wines made there represent a triumph of Teutonic tenacity and skill pitted against overwhelming odds.

The grape varieties, numbering less than a dozen, are of prime importance. The *Riesling* is by far the best, and all great German wines are made with it. The extensive plantings in the Rheingau and along the Mosel produce wines of unique character. The *Sylvaner* is softer and milder than the Riesling, yielding twice as much per acre than that small-yield aristocratic variety. The *Gewürztraminer,* or *Traminer,* has finesse and an unmistakeable spiciness, quite pronounced in German plantings but considerably diminished in plantings abroad.

The wine-growing districts, as shown on the map opposite, are: the *Palatinate,* or *Pfalz,* the largest producer of the four major districts; the *Rheingau,* the smallest, but producing the largest number of truly great wines; the *Rheinhessen,* almost the size of the Pfalz; and the *Mosel-Saar-Ruwer* area, which produces the most delicate wines in all Germany.

German wine buffs like to drink the wines at any time, not exclusively with meals or snacks. The wines are particularly good with pork *Delikatessen* specialties, fowl, fish, and seafood.

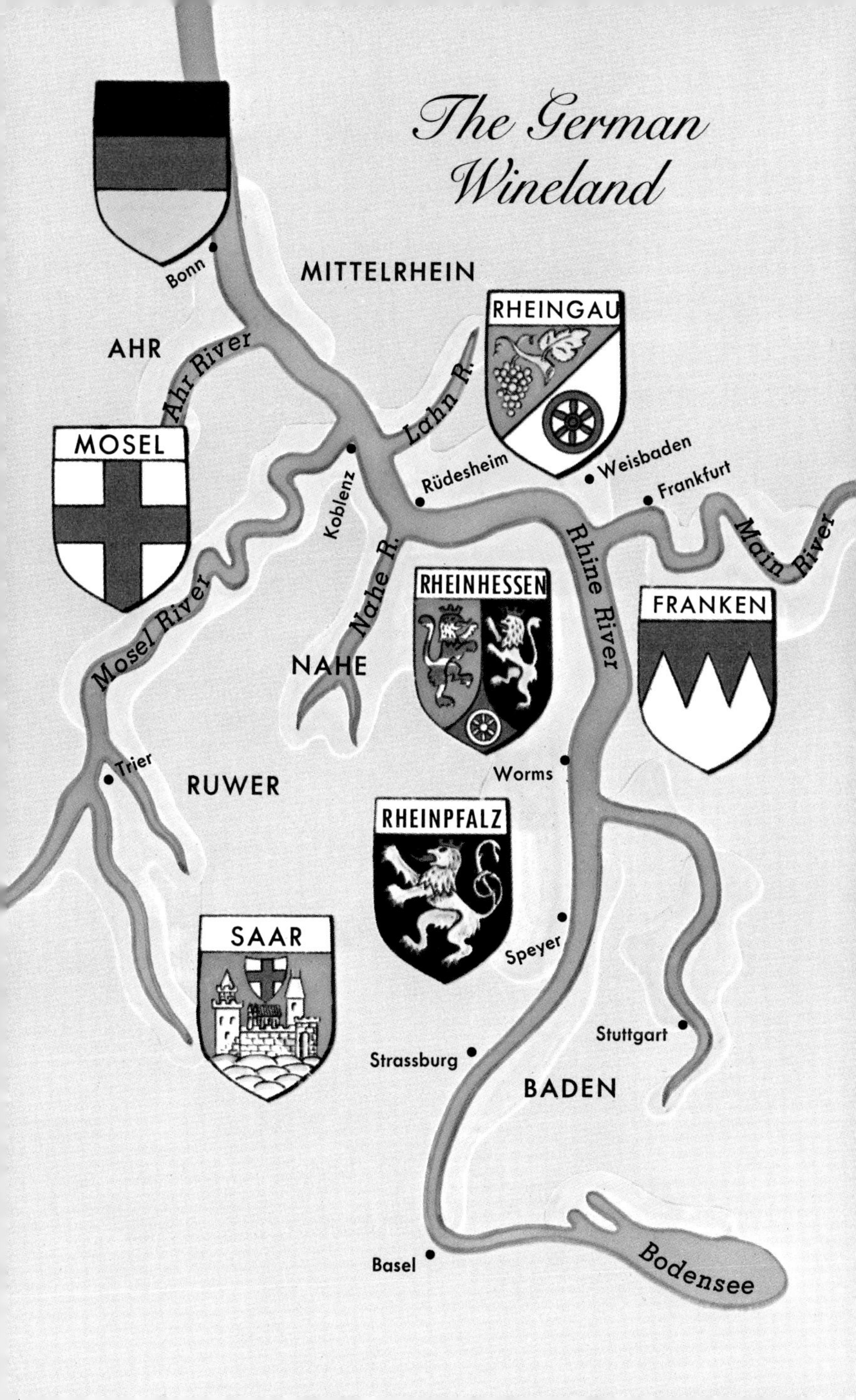
The German Wineland
Bonn
MITTELRHEIN
RHEINGAU
AHR
Ahr River
Lahn R.
MOSEL
Koblenz
Rüdesheim
Weisbaden
Frankfurt
Rhine River
Main River
Nahe R.
RHEINHESSEN
FRANKEN
Mosel River
NAHE
Trier
RUWER
Worms
RHEINPFALZ
SAAR
Speyer
Stuttgart
Strassburg
BADEN
Basel
Bodensee

GERMAN WINE LAWS, though strict, are augmented by the quality-control activities of the *Verband Deutscher Naturwein-Versteigerer,* the German Wine Association. The law, in true German style, goes into meticulous details, sometimes bordering on the ludicrous but giving the consumer a large measure of protection.

THE RECENT LABEL LAWS, evidenced on the 1972 labels, add more information while simplifying it for the consumer.

There are now three quality classes of German wine:

1. **Table Wine** *(Deutscher Tafelwein),* simple, pleasant everyday wines made from approved grape varieties in delineated areas. The label shows the name of the region but *not* the vineyard.

2. **Quality Wine of Designated Regions** *(Qualitätswein bestimmter Anbaugebiete).* Above average in quality, made from approved grape varieties in designated regions, this wine can carry the name of the village, vineyard, or specific area. A control number, appearing on the label, is assigned by the state agency.

3. **Quality Wines with Special Attributes** *(Qualitätswein mit Prädikat).* This is the highest classification, granted to the best German wines. A control number is assigned each wine and appears on the label with these other attributes:

Kabinett: Wine made only from fully matured grapes, without added sugar, in limited districts.

Spätlese: Wine made from grapes that have been "late picked" after harvest, giving more flavor, fruitiness, and delicacy to the wine.

Auslese: Wine made from only the best bunches of grapes, which are selected and pressed separately.

Beerenauslese (berry selection) and *Trockenbeerenauslese* (dry berry selection) indicate that the grapes used in the wine making have reached the highest degree of concentration of sugar and flavor.

Every quality wine must list the bottler *(Abfüller),* and if the wine is bottled by the producer-owner the label will state: *Erzeugerabfüllung* (bottled by the producer) and *aus eigenem Lesegut* (from the producer's own grapes).

A typical German wine label for a superior wine bearing the information required by the new labeling laws. Note the control number.

THE GREAT REGIONS, followed by the most important place-names and the outstanding *vineyards* in each region, are listed below:

THE RHEINGAU

Eltville—*Sonnenberg, Langenstück.*
Erbach—*Marcobrunn, Siegelsberg, Steinmorgen.*
Geisenheim—*Rothenberg.*
Hallgarten—*Deutelsberg, Schönell.*
Hattenheim—*Steinberg, Nussbrunnen, Wisselbrunnen.*
Hochheim—*Domdechaney.*
Johannisberg—*Schloss Johannisberg, Hölle, Klaus.*
Kiedrich—*Gräfenberg, Wasserrose.*
Oestrich—*Eiserberg.*
Rauenthal—*Baiken, Gehrn.*
Rüdesheim—*Berg Bronnen, Berg Lay, Berg Burgweg, Berg Rottland.*
Winkel—*Schloss Vollrads.*

THE RHEINHESSEN

Bingen—*Eisel, Rochusberg, Rosengarten.*
Bodenheim—*Bock, Ebersberg.*
Dienheim—*Falkenberg.*
Nackenheim—*Engelsberg, Rothenberg.*
Nierstein—(collective names are now used).
Oppenheim—*Kreuz, Sacktrager.*

THE PFALZ

Bad Durkheim—*Michelsberg.*
Deidesheim—*Herrgottsacker, Grainhübel, Leinhöhle.*
Forst—*Kirchenstück, Jesuitengarten, Freundstück.*
Königsbach—*Bender, Idig.*
Ruppertsberg—*Hoheburg.*
Wachenheim—*Gerümpel, Bächel.*

THE MOSEL

Bernkastel—*Doktor, Lay.*
Brauneberg—*Juffer, Falkenberg.*
Erden—*Treppchen, Prälat.*
Graach—*Josephshof, Himmelreich.*
Piesport—*Goldtröpfchen, Lay.*
Urzig—*Würzgarten, Schwarzlay.*
Wehlen—*Sonnenuhr, Nonnenberg.*
Zeltingen—*Himmelreich, Schlossberg.*

CONNOISSEURS OF GERMAN WINES who delight in the fragrant subtleties of the great vintages—and who can afford them—have a tendency to look down their noses at two very popular wines, *Liebfraumilch* and *Moselblümchen*. Nonetheless these two imports are the best-known German wines in the United States, and while there are a number of rather poor examples, some certainly do not deserve the contemptuous attitude accorded them by critics—and by wine snobs.

LIEBFRAUMILCH means "Milk of the Blessed Mother," and was originally the wine of Liebfrauenkirche and Worms. The name is now used for any wine, or blend, from almost anywhere in Germany. Most often it is a product of Rheinhessen or the Pfalz. Some shippers market very good wines from Nierstein, Oppenheim, Nackenheim, and other regions as *Liebfraumilch*.

The name of the shipper, and sometimes that of the producer, is the consumer's most reliable guide to the quality of the wine. Occasionally a *Liebfraumilch* label will also specify that it is *Spätlese* or *Auslese*, an additional indication of better than average quality. Good *Liebfraumilch* is very pleasant, particularly in summer when its lightness is best appreciated.

MOSELBLÜMCHEN means "Flower of the Mosel" and is the name given to the lesser wines of the Mosel Valley. Like *Liebfraumilch*, it is usually a blend, with some sugar added, and somewhat lighter and more fragrant. The principal grape used is the *Sylvaner*. It is never estate-bottled, and the consumer's best guide to its quality is the name of the shipper.

FRANKENWEIN is made from a variety of grapes and is often the best buy in the cheaper German wines. It is sold in the stubby *Bocksbeutel*. The most famous slope, the *Steinberg*, has become synonymous with *Frankenwein*. The name *Steinwein* is properly applied only to the wines of Würzburg, the capital of the region.

LUXEMBOURG

About twenty miles of the eastern border of the tiny Grand Duchy of Luxembourg is formed by the Moselle River as it flows from France into Germany. The pretty, gently rolling left banks are planted in some 3,000 acres of vineyards, mostly *Riesling, Sylvaner,* and *Elbling.* The production varies dramatically from year to year due to the changeable northern climate. The white wines resemble both the Alsatian and German Mosels, ranging from light and fragrant to velvety and elegant. The Luxembourgers wisely drink most of their delicious production, but more is being exported to the United States, where these wines are beginning to receive critical approval.

THE LABELS indicate the three types of legal designations for bottled Luxembourg wines:

1. *Vin de la Moselle Luxembourgeoise,* followed by the grape variety, categorizes the wines of ordinary quality.
2. *Place-name,* with vineyard name and grape variety, designates the middle category.
3. *Appellation Complète,* which corresponds to the French *Appellation Controlée,* is reserved for the finest wines. In this category the label must show the vintage year, place-name, grape variety, vineyard, and the grower's name and address. There are other exacting controls and official tasting tests to ensure consistent quality.

THE BEST WINES are usually those made of:

Riesling—Distinctive, full and elegant. From Wormeldange, Ehnen, Wintrage, Schengen, and Remich.

Traminer—Full, velvety, and spicy. From Ahn, Wellenstein, Schwebsingen, and Machtum.

Riesling and Sylvaner—Light, with a slight *Muscat* taste. From Wellenstein and Remerschen.

Pinots—Full and generous wines. They include *Auxerrois, Pinot Blanc,* and *Pinot Gris* varieties. From Wellenstein, Schengen, and Remerschen.

ITALY

It is said that Italy is one vast vineyard. Smaller than California, it produces more wine than any other country in the world, and is the third largest exporter. Italians are natural wine drinkers, with a per capita consumption of almost 30 gallons a year. Most Italians drink their wine casually, just as casually as many of their vintners grow the grapes and make the wine. But there are an increasing number of exceptions to this easy-going attitude, and Italian wines are getting better all the time. Improved controls have helped.

Most of the billion gallons produced each year is quite ordinary, much of it pleasant, some excellent, and a little which can be classed as great.

Almost all Italian wines are named after the grape variety used, the name of the town, or the district of origin. Labeling is usually dependable, except for vintage indication. The Italians remain casual about vintage years, considering them of little importance. Carefully made wines are more subject to discernible variations from year to year than the more ordinary wines made with typical Italian abandon.

The important wine regions of Italy include: the *Abruzzi,* on the Adriatic; *Apulia,* the great southern plain; *Calabria;* the *Campania* around Naples; *Latium; Lombardy; Piedmont,* home of some superb wines; *Umbria, Trentino-Alto Adige, Tuscany, Veneto, and Sicily.*

Since one out of every eight acres has vines on it, the whole map of Italy, on the facing page, could be colored with a vinous tint. The place of origin of the better-known wines is indicated by the numerals keyed to the list of their names. The principal regions are shown in capital letters. A few of the famous Italian cities are shown for the reader's orientation.

The Wines of Italy
VALLE D'AOSTA
9
PIEDMONT
3
Asti
LOMBARDY
4
TRENTINO ALTO ADIGE
Venice
VENETO
LIGURIA
EMILIA ROMAGNA
7
11
Florence
TUSCANY
6
14
2
MARCHES
15
Adriatic Sea
UMBRIA
8
LATIUM
Rome
5
ABRUZZI
CAMPANIA
CAPRI
10
Naples
BASILICATA
1
APULIA
CALABRIA
Palermo
12
SICILY
13
THE BETTER-KNOWN WINES:
Aglianico del Vulture 1
Aleatico 2
Asti Spumante 3
Barbera 3
Barbaresco 3
Bardolino 4
Barolo 3
Castelli Romani 5
Chianti 6
Cinque Terre 7
Est! Est!! Est!!! 8
Frascati 5
Gattinara 9
Lacrima Christi 10
Lambrusco 11
Marsala 12
Moscato 13
Orvieto 8
Sangiovese 14
Soave 4
Valpolicella 4
Verdicchio 15

GOVERNMENT CONTROLS, instituted in Italy in 1963, have gone a long way toward correcting the nonchalant attitude toward nomenclature which prevailed until then. The lack of safeguards for place-names, combined with haphazard methods of viticulture and viniculture, had relegated Italian wines to a lower status than they deserved. Today the new controls, both governmental and self-imposed, and a more serious attitude toward wine making, are building up the reputation of Italian wines at home and abroad.

Three denominations of origin controls have been established in Italy:

1. **Simple** *Denominazione di Origine Simplice* is for ordinary wines grown traditionally in a decreed area. This carries no quality rating.
2. **Controlled** *Denominazione di Origine Controllata* is reserved for wines meeting stipulated standards of quality.
3. **Controlled and Guaranteed** *Denominazione di Origine Controllata e Garantita* is given only to fine wines meeting quality and price standards set by government agencies. Once awarded, the recipient is under continuous control.

Contrary to popular notion, all red Italian wine does not taste like Chianti. There is a wealth of taste differences ranging from the majestic *Barolo* through the subtleties of aged *Chianti Classico* to the light, fragrant *Valpolicella*. The rosés are light and fresh, delightful when young.

The whites run a great gamut of taste, dry through sweet, some light, some big-bodied.

Besides the famed Vermouths, excellent and unique dessert wines, with a full range of taste characteristics, are also made in Italy. Sparkling *(spumante),* and slightly sparkling *(frizzante)* wines have a special charm.

VOLUNTARY CONTROLS are exercised through the National Institute for the Inspection of Denomination of Origin *(Institutione del Comitato Nazionale per la Tutela delle Dominazione di Origine).* For example, the *Instituto Nazionale per l'Esportazione (I.N.E.)* awards this familiar seal to Italian wines authorized for export.

Some of the best wines of Italy, listed by region, include:

ABRUZZI—*Montepulciano,* red; *Trebbiano,* white.

CALABRIA *Cirò di Calabria,* red; *Greco di Girace,* sweet white.

CAMPANIA—*Falerno,* red and white; *Lacrima Christi,* white.

EMILIA-ROMAGNA — *Lambrusco* and *Sangiovese,* both reds.

LATIUM—The wines of the *Castelli Romani,* dry whites, are considered among Italy's best. *Frascati* and *Est! Est! Est!* are the best known.

LOMBARDY—*Sassella, Grumello, Fracia* and *Inferno* are all reds. *Chiaretto* is an outstanding rosé.

LUCANIA (or Basilitica)—One of the best wines of southern Italy is the red Aglianico del Vulture.

PIEDMONT—The great *Barolo* and *Barbaresco* are Italy's finest reds. *Freisa, Barbera, Gattinara, Grignolino* and *Nebbiolo,* all cousins to the great pair, are products of this fine wine region, along with the sparkling, sweet *Asti Spumante.*

TRENTINO-ALTO ADIGE—Mostly whites made of *Riesling* and *Traminer* varieties.

TUSCANY—Home of the true and best *Chianti* and the sweet white *Vin Santo.*

UMBRIA—*Orvieto,* considered the best white in Italy, is now made dry as well as sweet.

SARDINIA—The best are the *Muscats* and *Malvasias,* sweet or fortified dessert wines.

SICILY—White *Mamertino,* red *Faro,* white and red *Corvo di Casteldaccia* and *Etna.* The best is the superb *Marsala.*

VENETO—The best of the region are the wines of Verona, the red *Valpolicella, Valpantena,* and *Bardolino,* and the smooth dry white *Soave.*

ELBA—The sweet and generous *Aleatico di Portoferraio* is a great dessert wine.

SPAIN

Almost four million acres, or better than one-tenth of the total area of Spain, is planted in vineyards. The yield is approximately 500 million gallons of wine each year. This is a relatively small yield in proportion to the total acreage. The reason for the limited production is the country's arid climate.

Sherry is the most famous Spanish wine but represents only a tiny percentage of the total amount of wine produced. It is a unique wine, made, blended, and aged by special processes, and is completely different from all other Spanish wines.

The best table wines are those made in the *Rioja* district, high upland country with severe winters. The reds here are better than the whites, and both bear a superficial resemblance to Bordeaux wines. Next to the Riojas are the wines of *Valdepeñas,* a major wine district south of Madrid. The region of *Andalusia,* at the southern end of Spain, is the producer of the famed *Sherry* and of the superb *Málaga,* which is no longer the fashionable wine it once was.

Only a little sparkling wine, called *Xampán* and pronounced "Champagne," is produced. It is rather sweet and is made southwest of Barcelona.

Spanish wines are usually inexpensive, representing a very good value for the price. Spanish wine controls, established some years ago, are being enforced more vigorously, and while a certain amount of rather inferior wines have been exported, the better ones are becoming more and more available. Spaniards are just as casual as the Italians when it comes to labeling for vintage years. The producer's name, or brand, is the best guide to the quality of the wine.

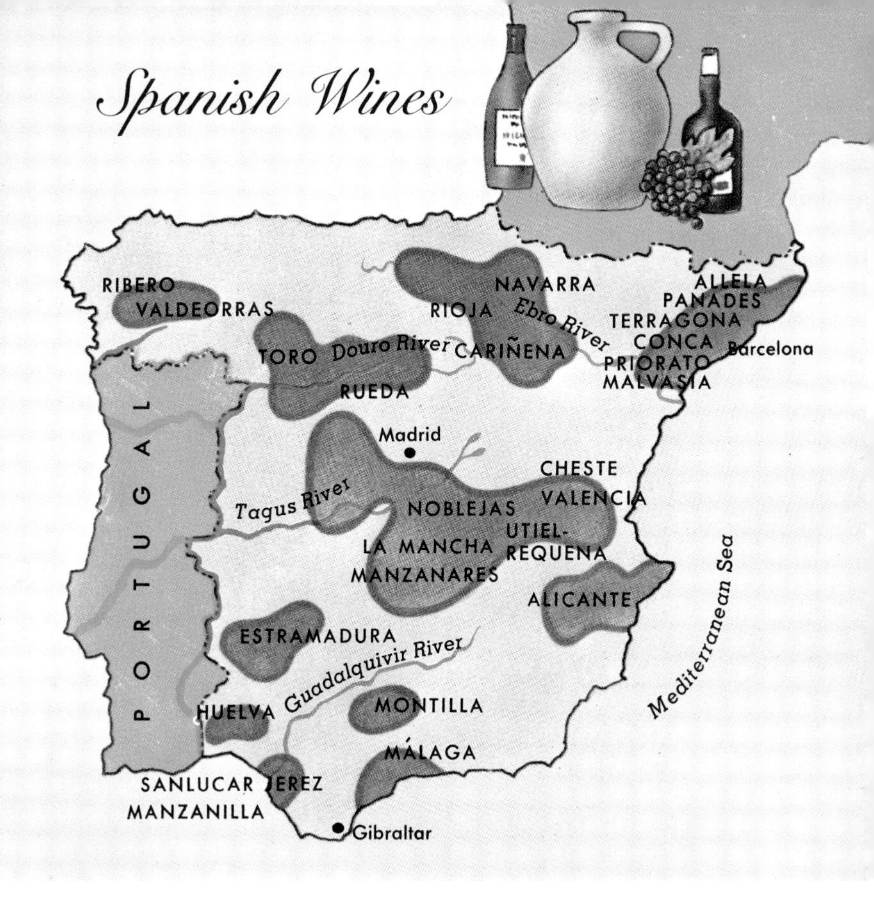

PLACE-NAMES, established under the regulations of the *Denominación de Origen*, are shown in the map.

ANDALUSIA—*Jerez or Xeres (Sherry); Montilla-Moriles; Málaga; Huelva; Monzanilla; Sanlúcar de Barrameda.*

CENTRAL SPAIN—*La Mancha; Noblejas; Manzanares.*

EAST COAST—*Malvasía de Sitges; Allela; Alicante; Tarragona; Priorato; Valencia; Panadés; Utiel-Requena; Cheste; Conca de Barbará; Barcelona.*

GALICIA—*Ribero; Valdeorras.*

NORTHERN SPAIN—*Cariñena Rioja; Navarra.*

WESTERN SPAIN—*Estramadura; Rueda; Toro.*

The landscape of Spain, one of picturesque and violent contrasts, is reflected in the great diversity of its wines. Spanish vintners are very skilled blenders, obtaining wines of pleasant characteristics from different vineyards and even from different parts of the country.

MUCH OF THE SPANISH VINEYARD land is parcelled out, and the number of small properties is so great as to defy official computation. The small plots are not suitable for mechanization, and most of their owners are too poor to afford more than the most rudimentary farm machines. The cooperative system was introduced, and there are now some 700 to 800 operating cooperatives. The bulk of production for export is wine shipped in the cask to England and Belgium.

Exports of Spanish wines to the United States have grown significantly in the past few years but, with the exception of sherry, bulk wines are still the major export.

Some of the most important Spanish firms exporting table wines to the New World and to other countries are: René Barbier; J. de Berger; Bodegas Bilbainas; Bodega El Faro; Bodega Torres; Bodega Riojanas; Bodegas La Rioja Alta; Castell del Bosch; Lopez Heredia; Marqués de Murrieta; Marqués de Riscal; and Mompó.

SANGRIA, a wine punch whose ingredients may vary at the whim of the maker, is usually a refreshing mixture of red wine, citrus fruit juices, sugar, and soda water. A popular hot weather drink in Spain, it has met with great success in the U.S., where several Spanish brands are imported.

TRUE SHERRY is made only in the strictly delimited district around the charming Andalusian town of Jerez de la Frontera. "*Sherry*" is the Anglicized pronunciation of Jerez. The principal grape used is the Palomino. After fermentation the wine is allowed to remain in the same vats. There the yeast causing the initial fermentation forms a film, called *flor,* on the surface of the wine, and produces a variety of pleasantly odorous products and aldehydes. The wine has now become *flor sherry,* or *Fino,* one of the two major classifications of sherry.

If a film does not form, or is prevented from forming by the addition of wine spirits to bring the wine to an alcohol content of 18% or more, it will become an *Oloroso,* the other major classification.

Both Finos and Olorosos undergo a good deal of blending and aging before they are ready for market.

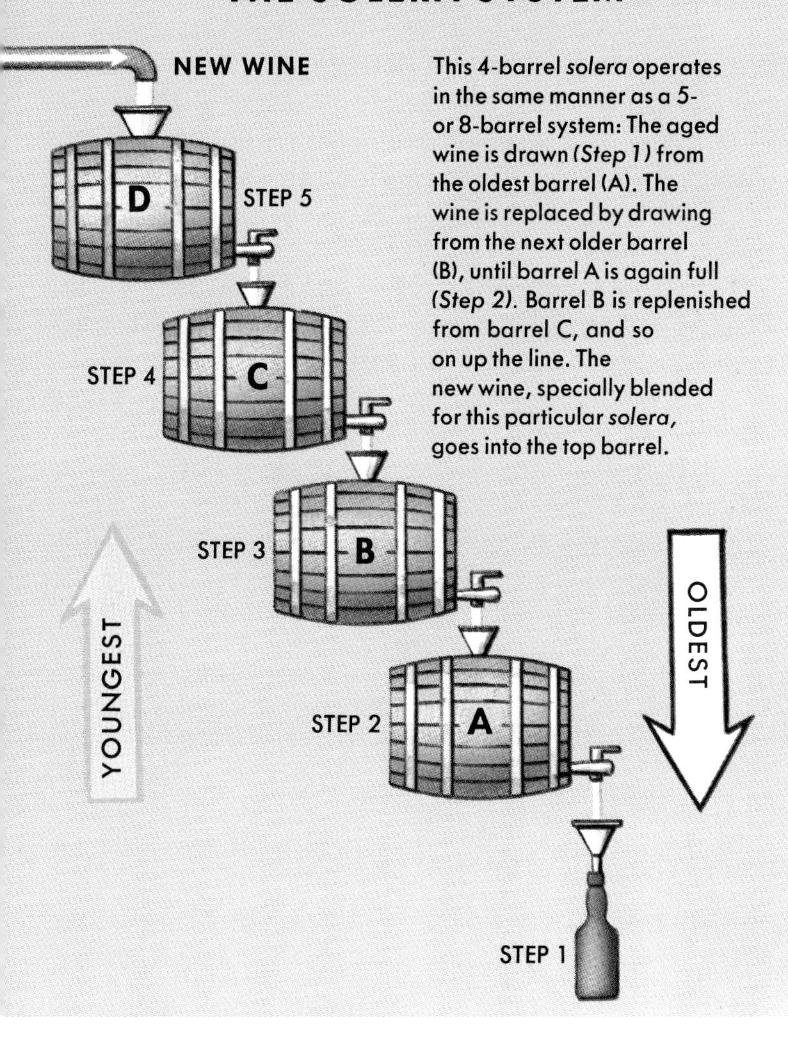

THE SOLERA SYSTEM is the agent whereby sherries are simultaneously aged and blended. It creates the uniformity of quality and of type of the various Spanish sherries that remains consistent year after year. *Fino soleras* remain at about the same alcoholic strength, but *oloroso soleras* will often reach higher concentrations, going as high as 22%. The *finos* are dry and pungent, the *olorosos* sweet and creamy.

PORTUGAL

Just as Spain is popularly known for its Sherry, Portugal is known for its *Port,* the most famous of all dessert wines. A bare 2% of all Portuguese wine is Port, and more than half of it is exported. *Madeira,* a favorite of our Colonial forbears, is no longer popular in the United States.

The most important table wines are the *Vinhos Verdes,* called "green wines" because of their fresh liveliness; the *Dãos,* full-bodied red and white wines; *Colares,* a very pleasant light red wine; and the somewhat sweet *Bucelas,* a white wine made near Lisbon. The Portuguese rosés and sparkling rosés have become very popular in the United States.

The better Portuguese wines carry the official Certificate of Origin, like the French *Appellation d'Origine,* and include: *Bucelas, Carcavelos, Colares, Dão, Moscatel de Setúbal,* and *Verde.*

THE VINHO VERDE vineyards are most unusual in that the vines grow on trees or high trellises, the land use being at a high premium.

The wines are light, with an average alcohol content between 8 and 11%, and a bit of bubbly effervescence which is very pleasant and refreshing. They are beginning to be exported in significant quantities.

The Moscatel de Setúbal can only be made in the boroughs of Setúbal and Palmela. A Frenchman once described it as "bottled sunlight." It is fortified with brandy and lighter than *Málaga.*

THE DÃO WINE vines are protected by mountain ranges shielding them from the seaborne winds and the inland heat. The soil is mainly granitic, the climate far from ideal, but the wines are smooth and suave. The full-bodied reds have an alcohol content of 12%, a velvety taste and a beautiful ruby red color.

The lemony-colored white wines are light, aromatic and fresh.

THE COLARES WINES grow in one of the loveliest touristic regions of Portugal, with a range of hills on one side and the Atlantic Ocean on the other. The vines grow in sandy ground, with roots going deeply down into very old strata. Planting vines often requires digging to a depth of nine to ten feet. In addition, reed screens must be erected to protect the vines from the winds blowing in from the Atlantic. The resulting wines have been described as "having a feminine complexion but a virile energy."

CARCAVELOS WINES are high in alcohol content, averaging 19%, and they are seldom exported from Portugal today.

BUCELAS WINES, rather rare outside Portugal itself, are best well aged, with increased bouquet and rich gold color.

Granjo is a sweet white wine whose sweetness comes from the *Botrytis cinera,* or noble rot, allowed to develop on the late-picked grapes, the same method used for Sauternes and Spätlese.

Almost 8% of the arable land of Portugal is devoted to vineyards. The variations of soil and the Atlantic climate produce a great variety of table wines, as well as the famous fortified wines. The principal wine-growing areas are shown in red on the map.

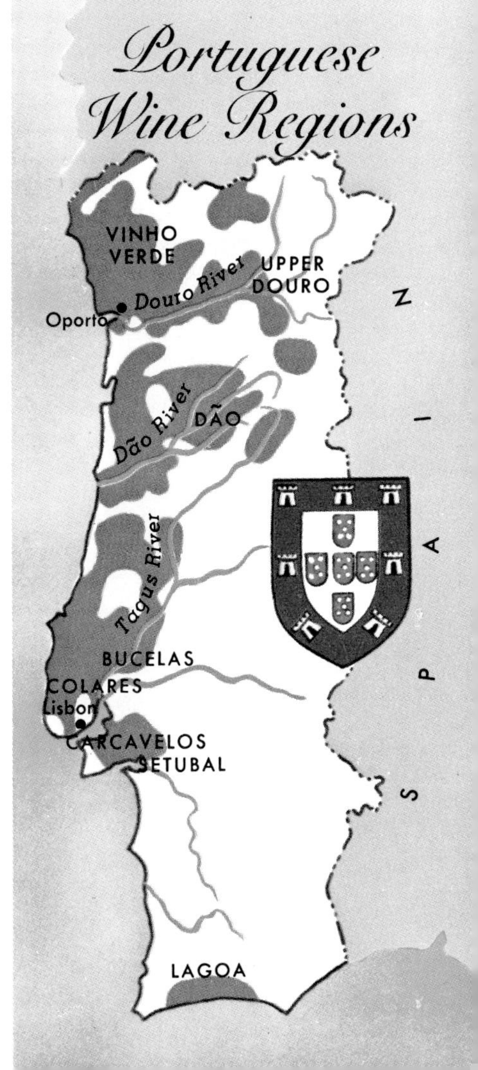

PORT, by both Portuguese and British law, is the wine made in the Upper Douro region, fortified by the addition of Portuguese grape brandy and shipped from Oporto, the seaport which has given the wine its name. Over 90% is exported, much of it to Scandinavia, some to France and England, and very little to the U.S.

THE VINIFICATION of Port differs from other wines in that it is arrested at some carefully determined point, about halfway in the fermentation process, by drawing off the juice into casks containing grape brandy.

This arrested fermentation produces a sweet wine with a 19 to 21% alcohol content.

The following year the wine is sent in Port "pipes," casks containing 138 gallons, to the wine lodges across the river from Oporto.

In a great year the maker may decide to make *Vintage Port*. In that case the wine will be shipped, usually to England, and bottled immediately. Vintage Ports are aged in the bottle for ten to fifteen years, sometimes more. They are expensive.

WINE NOT RESERVED for Vintage Port is blended and matured in oaken casks. The blending is a delicate, even inspired, operation resulting in a true-to-type wine for a particular brand, but different from every other brand.

As this wine ages it first becomes *Ruby Port,* then with more aging becomes *Tawny Port,* a wine of great elegance.

Port made from white grapes is, not surprisingly, called *White Port*. Ruby and White Ports are sometimes blended together to make Tawny Port.

True *Tawny Port* is aged in wood to acquire great elegance.

GREECE

This ancient land of wine has the climate and soil to produce wines that should live up to the legendary nectars Homer praised. That is not the case, however, at present, but there is hope that new regulations and controls, aided by the Institute of Tasters, will significantly improve the overall quality of Greek wines.

Greek wine makers may be divided into three main groupings: small individual producers; cooperatives; large private companies.

The *Peloponnesus* is the largest wine district, accounting for a quarter of the total production. Next in size is *Attica,* accounting for 15% of the total. The balance is produced by the islands of *Crete, Samos,* and *Santorin,* and the region of *Macedonia.*

Some of the best Greek wines come from the Peloponnesus, notably the luscious *Mavrodaphne.* The best white wine in Greece is reputed to be that of a small estate, *Pallini,* in Attica. An outstanding sweet wine, the *Muscat of Samos,* is made on the island of that name. Samos is one of the few place-names protected by Greek law.

RETSINA is a name which seems to appear on almost every bottle of Greek wine. It is not the name of a type of wine, but simply means that the wine, either rosé or white, has been treated with pine resin. The red wines do not receive this strange flavoring.

Greeks, particularly those of the central and southern parts of the country, seem to be genuinely fond of the taste. Those who dislike it, here or there, say it reminds them of turpentine. Tourists "going native" profess a great liking for it.

There are many theories, most defying conclusive proof, of how the *retsina* flavoring came about. The most prevalent one is that the ancient Greeks preserved their wine by using pine gum and got accustomed to the taste.

Those who like it say it should be drunk cool. Those who don't, say skip it.

AUSTRALIA

The great subcontinent of Australia is so unique in its fauna and flora that it is not surprising that Australian wines have a distinct character, their own peculiarities, and their own virtues. They have strange, wonderful names which heighten their individuality.

Australia's wine history starts in 1788 when the first vines, carefully transported, were planted in earth which had never nourished any kind of grape.

As in the other new world of America there were false starts, disasters and successes. Until 1820 wine making in Australia was a rich man's hobby. In that year the first commercial vineyard was started by the pioneering John Macarthur. From that moment, encouraged by his success, vines were planted in the Barossa Valley, in Berri and Rutherglen, the Swan Valley, Corowa, and the Hunter, Murray, and Eden valleys.

Almost every type of wine is produced. Because of the ethnic groups originally settling this great country, the proportion of wine types produced reflects the preferences of Anglo-Saxon taste.

Canada and Great Britain are the best customers for Australian wine at present. The American market is new but seems promising. Until the mid-1960's fortified and dessert wines led Australian wine production, but now the lead has been taken by table wines, the best wines made there today.

Almost half the total production is distilled as brandy or alcohol. Much is used in making the fortified wines.

The wine industry in the Pacific new world bears a resemblance to that of the American new world. The Australians have been quick to adapt technological advances and modern equipment to their wine-making procedures.

They, too, are operating their wineries and vineyards with a balanced mixture of the traditional and the new.

As the market for Australian wine grows, expansion brings more shiny stainless steel equipment into handsome modern plants, and new vineyards are planted with an eye to modern harvesting and cultivation.

Most new plantings reflect the demand for more table wines.

As can be seen in the map, above, the wine-growing regions lie almost entirely in the southeastern corner of the continent. The two notable exceptions are Swan Valley in the state of Western Australia and Roma in the state of Queensland. The names of the other districts, keyed to the numbers on the map, are:

1. Hunter Valley
2. Rooty Hill
3. Muswellbrook
4. Mudgee
5. Murrumbidgee Valley
6. Swan Hill
7. Robinvale
8. Murray Valley
9. Rutherglen Wahgunyah-Corowa
10. Tahbilk
11. Shepparton
12. Glenrowan-Milawa
13. Great Western
14. Southern Vales
15. Langhorne Creek
16. Coonawarra
17. Barossa Valley
18. Clare-Watervale
19. Adelaide Metropolitan
20. Swan Valley
21. Roma

The new, modern winery of the Rothbury Estate, which won the Royal Australian Institute of Architects' award, is in the Hunter River valley of the state of New South Wales. It is surrounded by a vineyard of more than a thousand acres.

The old, handsome buildings of the Seppelt winery at Seppeltsfield, in the Barossa Valley of the state of South Australia, stand on the site of the original winery established in 1851. Traditional methods are a hallmark of this winery.

Generic names, such as *Burgundy, Chablis,* and *Hermitage,* are on Australian wine labels but are usually written in smaller type than the regional or proprietary names which precede them—for example, *Chalambar Burgundy.* The use of the generic name is to be taken only as a general guide for a category of taste.

Varietal names are on the increase, in keeping with the growing interest in table wines. The British influence shows in the number of wines labeled as *Claret* and *Hock,* the latter used for Rhine-type wines. Australian reds are generally sturdy and deep in color. The best of them are smooth, with a pronounced vinous flavor. The Clarets come very close to the characteristics of their original Bordeaux forebears. The Burgundy-type reds bear very little resemblance to their French models, but are good enough to stand on their own merit alone.

The quality of the whites seem to vary much more than that of the reds. Some are light to the point of being thin, and some are as robust as the reds. Three general types dominate the whites: the *sauternes,* ranging from semi-sweet to sweet; the *chablis,* usually quite dry and big-bodied; and the *hocks,* or *rieslings.* The best of the latter are light and fragrant, usually dry. The *rosés* can be remarkably big in flavor and body. The versatile soil produces, in different regions, completely different wines.

Most Australian vintners make some sparkling wines. Some are made by the traditional in-the-bottle fermentation, or Champenois process, and some use one of the bulk fermentation processes. The bottle-fermented wines are generally better and also more expensive than those produced by bulk fermentation.

Variety, rather than specialization, seems to be the rule in Australia. Most vintners produce as wide a selection of wines—still, fortified, and sparkling—as possible. The climate and soil lend themselves to this multiplicity of wine types.

The same vine, planted in different parts of the wine-growing regions, will result in wines of very different and distinct character.

Very little Australian wine is exported as yet to the United States. The House of Seppelt is one of the pioneers in exporting these unusual and distinctive wines to our shores. We can look forward to an increase over the next few years.

Some of the leading brands are: S. Wynn & Co., Penfolds, Saltram, Lindeman's, Yalumba (S. Smith & Son), McWilliam's, Gramp's Orlando, Kaiser Stuhl, and Angove's. All are in the southeast corner of the country and offer a wide selection of table, dessert, and sparkling wines. Chateau Tabilk and McLaren Vale do not make fortified wines.

Australians are anxious to have their wines judged on their own merits, without comparison—just as one would not compare the waratah flower of New South Wales with an English rose.

CANADA

Canada's relatively small wine production and per capita consumption have both been growing steadily over the past ten years. The home-grown grapes are mostly *Vitis labrusca* varieties, with more hybrids being added every year. Wine grapes are also imported in significant quantities from the United States. A sizable amount of wine is made from fruits and berries other than grapes. Very little Canadian wine is exported to the U.S.; Canadians are so fond of their own product that they drink most of it themselves, and supplement it with imports.

In general, Canadian wine is light, fragrant, and very pleasant. There do not seem to be any *great* Canadian wines as yet, but there are many fine, delightful ones, as can be attested by the many tourists who have visited our great neighbor to the north.

A refreshing honesty and lack of pompous pretension is evidenced in these Canadian wine labels, representing most of the Canadian wine companies. With few exceptions a wine will be called just what it is: a red wine is labeled *Red Wine,* and it is described as dry, semi-dry, semi-sweet, or sweet, usually in English and French.

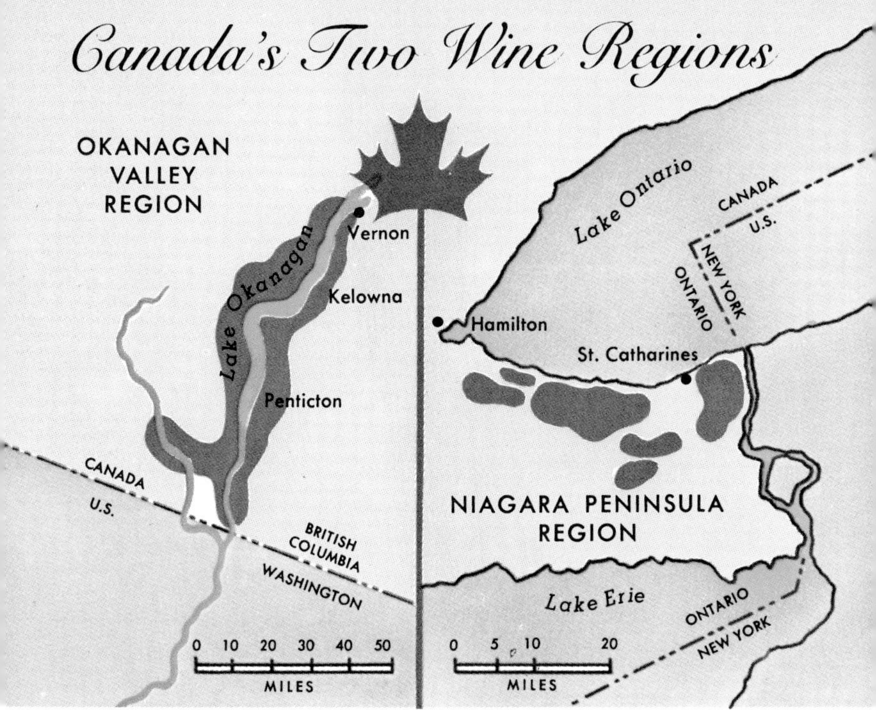

Canada's wine-growing areas are: **1.** the Niagara Peninsula, which grows 80% of the grapes used in Canadian wines, and **2.** the Okanagan Valley of British Columbia. Despite their northern location, both have more sunshine than many of the world's renowned vineyards. Please note the different "Scale of Miles" on the maps.

The principal wineries of Ontario are: Barnes, the oldest; Bright's, the largest; Castle; Chateau Cartier; Chateau-Gai; Jordan; London; and Turner.

British Columbia's include: Andrés; Growers'; Villa; Calona; Casabello; and Uncle Ben's.

In other parts we find: Castle in Saskatchewan; Danforth in Manitoba; and Andrés and Chalet in Alberta.

Most of them offer a complete selection of still, sparkling, and fortified wines.

Canada does not produce "vintage" wines. Climatic conditions in the grape-growing regions are relatively stable, making for grapes of good, even quality each year. The wines of different years' harvests are often blended to obtain a consistent character and quality.

Canadian wines are aged at the wineries in a variety of containers of the wine makers' choice until ready for shipment. There is comparatively little aging in the bottle.

HUNGARY

Wine making has always been a great tradition in Hungary, along with love-making to the romantic music of sobbing gypsy violins.

Wine-making standards are claimed to be among the highest, and Hungary pioneered the regulations affecting place-names and varietal regulations.

Top quality Hungarian wines are classified as *First Great Growths,* subject to stringent controls, or *Great Growths,* subject to less stringent controls. The controls are exercised at the source and there is no notation on the label. Except for *Tokay* and a very few others, classified wines carry the name of the grape variety preceded by the place name.

The most important white wine grape is the *Furmint,* used in making the great Tokay and a number of other superb Hungarian white wines. The outstanding red variety is the *Kadarka,* which produces most of the high quality red wines and is one of the varieties blended in the famous *Egri Bikavér,* or Bull's Blood.

TOKAY, or *Tokaj* in Hungarian, is Hungary's greatest wine and one of the world's greatest too. It is as unique as France's Château d'Yquem and Germany's greatest Trockenbeerenauslesen.

Its uniqueness is the product of a combination of a grape, the *Furmint,* which responds ideally to the climatic condition, a volcanic soil with elements of feldspar, clay, and porphyry, and a special method of vinification. The soil is considered so precious that no one from outside is allowed into the growing area.

The Tokay-Furmint grape is allowed to become overripe, developing the *Botrytis* mold, concentrating the sugars to a maximum. Since berries ripen unevenly in a cluster, the overripe berries are separated and placed in baskets called *puttonys.*

When *Aszu Tokay* is made, a given number of puttonys are added to the ripe berry run. The number of puttonys is shown on the neck label of the bottle. The larger the number, (from 3 to 5) the more concentrated the wine.

Tokay Szamorodni is a full-bodied white wine made either dry or sweet. Like Aszu Tokay, it comes from *Furmint* grapes but the berries are not segregated, the whole vineyard harvest being fermented together. There is no indication of puttony strength and the vintage year is an important factor.

Egri Bikavér, Bull's Blood of Eger, is the dramatic name of the best-known Hungarian red wine. It is dark and heavy, tends to be dry, and well-aged. Good vintage years develop a velvety smoothness blended with its fieriness. It is a blend of the *Kadarka, Médoc Noir* and *Burgundi* grape varieties.

Debröi Hárslevelü is a golden sweet wine made from the Hungarian grape, *Hárslevelü.* It has been likened to a medium-quality Sauternes by some experts. On the shores of Lake Balaton, the largest European lake, are the vineyards producing some of the best Hungarian wines available in this country.

Badacsonyi Kéknyelü is the best known of that region. It is a dry, pale green wine which, in a good year, has a quality reminiscent of fine dry Moselle and Rhine wines.

Badacsonyi Szürkebarát, or Grey Friar of Badacsony, is a little sweeter, mellow and golden. It is made from the *Pinot Gris* grape variety.

Szekszárdi Vörös, a claret type, is typical of the best reds grown on the slopes near the Yugoslav border. It has a fine fragrance, is pleasantly dry, and is not too heavy. It was said to be one of Franz Liszt's favorite wines. While the Hungarian word *voros* is the English equivalent of Claret, the grape variety used is the *Kadarka.* The same grape is used for two other full-bodied reds: *Szekszárdi Kadarka* and *Villányi Kadarka.*

Despite their almost unpronounceable names, these are all wines which merit more than just a casual acquaintance.

AUSTRIA

The land of Strauss waltzes, *Sachertorte,* and Baroque architecture has produced wine for nearly a thousand years. The better Austrian wines are predominantly white, light in alcohol, and fairly dry.

Austria is a wine-drinking country, and much of its wine is consumed within its borders. Not enough wine is made to quench the Austrian thirst, and imports, mainly from neighboring Italy, exceed exports. There are four wine-producing regions: *Lower Austria,* with more than 50,000 acres of vineyards; *Burgenland,* a southeastern province, once part of Hungary; *Styria,* bordering on Yugoslavia; and *Vienna* itself.

AUSTRIAN WINE LABELS show the name of the district or village of origin, sometimes the name of the individual vineyard, or the name of the grape variety. The notation *naturbelassen* indicates that the wine is a natural wine, unsweetened. *Gerebelt* means that the grapes are hand-picked.

The bottles are the long slender ones associated with German wine, and they are either green or brown.

THE GRAPES used in making the white wines include several types of Rieslings, such as *Rheinriesling, Riesling-Sylvaner,* and *Welsch-Riesling;* also *Furmint; Muscat-Ottonel; Grüner Veltliner,* and *Traminer.* For red wines the grapes include *Blaufränkisch; Blauburgunder; Sankt Laurent; Wildbacher,* and *Kadarka.*

THE WHITE WINES are generally the best. Among them should be noted: *Gumpoldskirschner,* a light, fragrant wine long a Viennese favorite; the *Sandweine* of the lake district of Burgenland; the still or sparkling wines of the Kloch district of Styria; and the *Grüner Veltliner* varietals of Vienna.

THE RED WINES, though rated lower than the white, are pleasant and unusual. Among the more interesting are the *Voslauer Rotwein,* from the Weinerwald-Steinfeld district; the fiery *Kadarka,* from Mattersburg; and the dark red Styrian *Schilcherwein.*

VIENNA'S little wine villages, now in its suburbs, produce pleasant wines drunk young at the source by Viennese and tourists in the wine gardens.

YUGOSLAVIA

The land of the southern Slavs produces about 125 million gallons of wine yearly and ranks, in production, with the United States and Greece. Exports more than doubled in the 1950's and continue to rise.

The country produces a large variety of wines from such imported vines as *Merlot, Riesling, Sauvignon, Sylvaner,* and *Traminer,* as well as from hybrids and many native varieties such as *Prokupac, Smedervka,* and *Ezerjo.* Most wines are blended and vintages are relatively unimportant. Yugoslav wines offer a great and varied range of taste, from the robust southern reds to the light freshness of the whites of Slovenia.

THE WINE-GROWING DISTRICTS are: *Serbia,* producing almost half of the total made in the country; *Croatia,* accounting for about 35%; *Slovenia* and *Macedonia,* less than 10% each. The district of *Bosnia-Herzegovina* produces a little wine. *Montenegro's* production is almost nil.

SERBIAN wines are mostly reds, some rosés, and a few whites. Not many are exported, but some of these names may become better known in the future: *Zupa,* for robust, heavy reds; *Krajina,* mostly reds, with one white, the *Bagrina* of *Krajina; Smederevo,* for good whites made from the *Smedervka* grape.

CROATIAN wines are of two types—those of the inland districts and those of the Adriatic coast. The inland slopes produce light, pleasant wines such as *Vinica, Varazdin,* and *Medjugorica.* The Adriatic vineyards produce big red wines, full of tannin, and with very little acid. They are usually labeled as varietals together with the place-name, such as "Plavac of Vis," made from the Plavac grape in the Vis region.

The wines of the Istrian Peninsula show a strong Italian influence. One of the better-known wines of that region is the Malvazya, made from the Italian Malvasia grape.

Most of the grape growing is done by peasant viticulturists whose holdings, limited by law to 25 acres, amount to 95% of the total area planted in vines. A few authorized exporters control wine exports to the Iron Curtain countries and the rest of the world.

THE SOUTHERN NEIGHBORS

MEXICO was the first country on the North American Continent to raise grapes from European stock, but it is not today a wine-drinking country. Some 40 companies make wines, both still and sparkling, or brandy from the 200,000 tons of grapes grown there annually. Mexicans have a per capita consumption of about a *half pint* of wine annually compared to, say the Italians' nearly 30 gallons! Mexican vinters are a hopeful lot, so that consumption of their product can only go UP!

The wine-growing regions of Mexico are in the northern part of the country. *Aguascalientes* is the most important. Among the other regions are *La Laguna, Delicias, Baja California, Saltillo, Chihuahua, Querétaro,* and *Torreón.*

The vineyards and wineries are primarily family affairs. Among the principal ones are: *Vinícola de Aguascalientes; Misión de Santo Tomás; Vinicola de Saltillo; Madero,* and *Vergel.* The latter is the youngest and fastest-growing winery.

THE ARGENTINIAN is indeed a wine drinker. His country ranks fourth among the world's wine producers, with an average yearly output of over 500 million gallons, and he drinks practically all of it! His consumption represents well over 22 gallons per capita.

The Spanish missionaries brought the vine to Argentina in 1566, but the development of the industry was left to the Italian immigrants. In the 19th Century they began irrigating the desert land of Mendoza and created a new vineland.

Two regions produce nearly all the wine: Mendoza, contributing about 70%, and San Juan, over 25%. Red wines far outnumber the whites and rosés, and vast quantities of vermouth are also produced. Sparkling wines are made by all three methods—bottle fermentation, bulk fermentation, and carbonation.

Right: An Argentinian vineyard, showing a typical method of trellising the vines. Note the wide alleys and foliage height.

Below: Argentine gauchos, in their costumes, parade in the festive *Vendimia,* the celebration of the grape harvest.

Argentine wine makers have chosen, with a few exceptions, to use modern mass-production methods to process the yield from their more than 600,000 acres of vineyards. Immense fermenting vats, some holding more than 250,000 gallons, are currently used. The rest of their wine-making equipment is on a corresponding scale.

This makes a lot of wine, quickly and economically, but it does not make for a very high-quality product. In producing such huge quantities, it is impossible to use the loving care and individual attention given to fine wines made in small lots.

However, there are some Argentine *bodegas* specializing in quality wines, carefully made in relatively smaller quantity.

The grape variety which dominates the red wine production is the *Malbec,* a French export from the Bordeaux region. It produces about two-thirds of all red wines in Argentina. The balance is made with other familiar European types, mostly Italian and French. The dominating grape for white wine is the *Criollas,* one of the varieties imported by the early missionaries. Other varieties include the Spanish *Pedro Ximénez, Malvasia, Pinot Blanc, Riesling, Sauvignon,* and *Sémillon.*

Argentina, like France and Germany, has established an excellent body of law regulating the bottling and labeling of its wines. The Argentine consumer is well protected against fraud and misrepresentation.

One section, which could be taken as a model by all other wine countries, forbids the use of famous place-names such as Chablis, Rhine, Bordeaux, etc., unless the wine is imported from that region. A place-name can be used only if the wine came from there and has its typical characteristics. No foreign wine may be blended with Argentine wine.

CHILE'S 275,000 acres of vineyards produce the best wines of South America, and rank it among the first dozen or so in world production. The soil and climate, combined with a good irrigation system, are good for the wine grape. A great tradition of careful wine making was left to the Chileans by the French, who planted the better vineyards.

No great wines have emerged as yet, but Chilean wines are greatly appreciated everywhere. They are very good and so reasonably priced that they constitute one of the best wine bargains.

There are three major wine growing areas: the *Northern Region,* where fortified wines dominate; the *Central Region,* specializing in good- and high-quality table wines, and the *Southern Region,* which produces ordinary table wines.

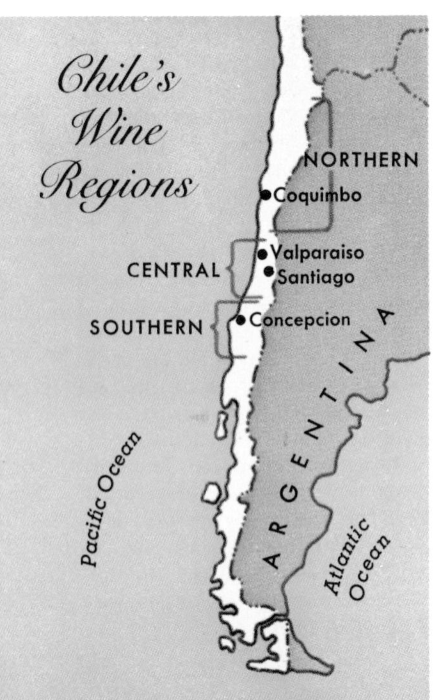

THE NORTHERN REGION, stretching some 350 miles, produces Chile's best table grapes and the wine grapes for fortified wines made to resemble Port, Madeira, or Sherry.

THE CENTRAL REGION, about 150 miles long, makes the country's best wines. The Aconcagua and Maipo River valleys produce the region's highest-quality wines. The Bordeaux influence is very strong, and the *Cabernet* grapes produce strong, stable red wines, well balanced and of distinctive finesse. Fine white wines are also made, mostly from *Pinot Blanc, Sauvignon,* and *Sémillon* grapes.

THE SOUTHERN REGION produces ordinary, everyday wines,

good but with little distinction. A little *Riesling* is made there. Chile's *Riesling* is one of its best white wines. When first sold in the United States, it was an outstanding bargain, priced under one dollar a bottle, and met with great approval. Despite its good reception abroad, however, Chilean vintners have cut Riesling production, finding it uneconomical to grow.

Other white wines are now made in greater quantities from such grape varieties as *Pinot Blanc, Sauvignon,* and *Sémillon.*

The wine industry in Chile is very strictly controlled. While some regulations are part of an attempt by the government to combat alcoholism, wine age controls and export rules protect the consumer abroad.

Excess production cannot be marketed in the country. Export is an obvious solution, but to prevent the dumping of inferior Chilean wines abroad the government has ruled that exported wines must have a minimum alcoholic content—12% for white, 11.5% for red—and all must be at least one year old. Export wines are also subject to age controls under four classifications: *Courant,* for one-year-old wines; *Special,* for two-year-old; *Reserve,* for four-year-old, and *Gran Vino,* for six-year-old or older.

Most of the exported wines carry the varietal names, and offer a good value.

BRAZIL, the largest country in South America, has almost 200,000 acres in vines. Because of the climate, Brazilian wine makers have planted mostly *Vitis labrusca* and American hybrids, with a few carefully tended European varieties. There has been a considerable expansion of the wine industry to meet the increasing internal demand. Very little is exported at present but the situation may soon change.

URUGUAY, the smallest country in South America, has a wine production almost equal to that of Brazil. The Uruguayan enjoys his wine; very little is exported. While Uruguay also uses North American hybrids, there are considerable plantings of European varieties such as *Cabernet, Barbera,* and *Nebbiolo.*

Most Uruguayan wines are named after the locality where they are made or after the varietal name.

. . . AND MORE DISTANT NEIGHBORS . . .

RUSSIA, always an important wine producer, is aiming at an annual production of over 250 million gallons. Most of the wine is grown and made in a vast crescent of southern Russia, from the frontiers of China and Mongolia to the Rumanian border. The finest wine region is the *Crimea,* whose small production is compensated by the quality of its sweet and dessert wines. The other important wine regions are in the Soviet Republics of *Armenia, Azerbaijan,* and *Georgia.* The amount of Russian wine exported to any country seems to be directly related to the political climate. With improved relations, more good Russian wines may reach the U.S. in the future.

The Russian taste, predominantly for sweet wines, extends to sparkling wines. The best is reputed to be the Crimean *Kaffia.* Near Rostov, in the Don Valley, the vineyards are important producers of both red and white sparkling wines.

Armenia makes large quantities of natural table wines, fortified wines, and brandies.

Place-names are regulated by state decree, although the designations permit using such names as Port, Tokay, and Madeira.

NORTH AFRICA, under French influence, became a major producer of wine, particularly in Algeria. In recent years, however, the wine industry in Algeria, under the control of the Moslem population, has deteriorated to a critical point. Tunisia continues normal production, and quality controls have been established. Morocco, whose wine industry accounts for one-quarter of its agricultural income, has inaugurated a sound program of controls from vine to finished product. Most North African wines are reds, heady and rough, although a few of good quality are produced in all of these three countries.

SOUTH AFRICA has an excellent climate for grape growing, but there has been little incentive to make good wine, since the population is more interested in hard liquor than wine. The country has had, for some time, the world's largest per capita consumption of alcohol. The wines were, until recently, extremely rough and devoid of distinction, but the picture is changing.

JAPAN'S wine industry is one of the world's newest, and, characteristically, the Japanese are industriously expanding it. Their hope is that wine drinking may check the drain on grain supplies caused by the enormous consumption of *sake* and beer made from grain.

The principal wine-growing regions are the districts of Osaka and Yamanashi, on the island of Honshu. While European, Asian, and American grape varieties can grow there, the acid soil and dampness are not conducive to the production of high-quality wine.

Typical Japanese vineyards and wineries are small. Their personnel are often inexperienced for while there is a great tradition in agriculture, there is none in wine making. However, if the history of other Japanese enterprises is a guide, the inquisitiveness and industriousness of the Japanese will work wonders. There are many cooperatives and large companies, such as the *Sado-ya* Cooperative in Yamanashi and *Suntory,* which are making significant progress in the production of pleasant wines from European and other grape varieties.

Generally, the dessert wines are more successful than the table wines.

Antiseptically-garbed Japanese girls harvest grapes in one of the Suntory vineyards. Note the overhead trellising, for maximum exposure to sunlight.

In the preceding chapters we have seen *how* wine is made, *where* it is made, and *who* makes it. The limitations of size and scope of this book make it a primer, covering as simply as possible the major highlights of wine lore. As in all human endeavors which have been refined through the ages, one need not be a professional wine taster to enjoy a glass of wine, any more than one need be an Olympic champion to enjoy sports or a virtuoso to enjoy playing a musical instrument. The degree of enjoyment normally increases as your knowledge and skill increases. You learn most about wines by drinking them, and what a pleasant study that is!

A list of suggested additional reading is included (page 154) for those who have been sufficiently intrigued to want more extensive guidance on the fascinating aspects of wine. And now we will explore the practical consumer arts of buying, storing, and using wine for maximum enjoyment.

SHOPPING for wine is basically the same as shopping for any other kind of food for your table. Your choice is guided primarily by your taste preference and your budget.

Assuming that you live in an area of reasonably convenient shopping facilities, you will normally go where you have confidence in the honesty and competence of the merchant. You have learned to trust his recommendations and you like the quality and choice range of his wines, which are probably displayed in an attractive and intelligent manner.

The above criteria apply to wine as they do to a roast, a basket of fruit, or any other foodstuffs. Your choice of food is determined by the occasion, and so should your choice of wine. A simple meal calls for a simple wine, a feast for a correspondingly festive vintage. There are staple wines, just as there are staple foods. Some wines are for consumption soon after purchase and some for storage, to be used at a later date when it will reach full maturity.

JUG WINES, in gallons and half-gallons, are generally of good quality, quite satisfactory for everyday use. They often offer the best value in the low-priced, readily available American table wines.

There is no advantage in storing these wines as they are ready to drink at the time of purchase, and are not likely to improve with age. By buying these larger containers and transferring the contents into assorted smaller bottles, you can save a little money and have a useful range of sizes for your table and kitchen.

Most American vintners make jug wines. Among those which have found wide acceptance are: *The Christian Brothers'* wines, bottled in fifths or jugs; *Charles Krug's CK* and *Mondavi Vintage* products; *Almaden's Mountain* wines and some generics; *Louis Martini's Mountain Red, White,* and *Rosé; Italian Swiss Colony's Chianti* and *Rosé; Gallo's Hearty Burgundy, Rhine Garten,* and *Paisano; Guild's Famiglia Cribari,* for rather sweet wines, *Vino de Tavola* for slightly drier and fuller wines, and the generics bottled under their *Winemasters* label; and *Paul Masson's* generics, bottled only in half-gallons. The above are all California wines.

In New York and other parts of the country vintners are likely to follow the lead of *Taylor, Great Western,* and *Gold Seal* in bottling their wines in larger containers. A few imports arrive as jug wines, particularly Spanish and Italian brands. The quality has been uneven, and varies from year to year. Some very good buys have appeared from time to time.

When exploring the jug wine field, the buyer should ascertain if the unknown wine which interests him is available in fifths, and if so, he should purchase the smaller bottle for testing. If no fifths are available, try the half-gallon. If you like the wine, the most economical way to buy it is by the case of four gallons, dividing the gallons into smaller screw-cap containers at home.

In buying better quality wines whose price is correspondingly higher, the consumer should look for more than the enjoyable, everyday drinking suitability of the inexpensive jug wine. The cost should be a guide to the degree of finesse, complexity of taste, and other quality characteristics.

Premium American wines, particularly the varietals, often offer the best bargain, dollar for dollar, compared with imports. If these wines are properly stored and aged in the consumer's wine cellar, they will often turn out to be spectacular values and far superior to the import of equal price at the time of purchase.

READ THE LABEL when buying any but a wine you know well. If you need help, ask the storekeeper. If he can't give you a satisfactory translation of the significant information you seek, don't buy the wine. Most countries require honest labeling and usually enforce it. Beware of too general descriptions and vague terminology.

HOW TO BECOME A SUCCESSFUL WINE SHOPPER:

1. Be adventurous. Take advantage of every opportunity to taste different wines. Attend winetastings whenever you can, or invite a few friends to a share-the-expense winetasting party at home. Go on wine-shopping sprees; it is not expensive, and is fun.

2. Learn to read labels. Elsewhere in this book you will find helpful pointers on reading foreign and American wine labels for pertinent information.

3. When trying a wine for the first time, buy small bottles, if available. Choose a size that you are likely to finish at one sitting. Few table wines will keep their attractiveness for more than a day once opened.

4. Try the low-priced wines as well as the more expensive ones. When you find a type to your taste, try several different brands in various price ranges before you buy in any large quantity.

5. Once you have found a wine you like, at a fair price, buy as much as you can store safely, and in proportion to your future needs. Be sure the wine is from the shipment you tasted and liked.

6. Learn something of the keeping characteristics of any wine you want to "put down" for a year or more. Remember: Whites usually have a short life; reds often improve with additional aging.

7. Keep a *cellar book* for labels and your notations on all wines you want to remember, either good or bad. You should note the date of purchase, price, dealer, date tasted, and your impressions of color, aroma, bouquet, taste, aftertaste, body, acidity, dryness, etc. Your notes can be as elaborate as you wish, including the food you had with the wine, or other people's opinions.

STORING WINE

Wine is stored by the consumer for a variety of good reasons—convenience, economy, and improvement of the wine itself. Whether his wine cellar is a closet in an apartment or a separate room in the basement, the benefits and the basic requirements apply.

The convenience of having a ready-to-drink assortment of wines at hand is obvious. Being able to buy wine at a good price and storing it for later use can be advantageous in times of rising prices.

Most wines, particularly the reds, benefit by additional aging. A wine of moderate appeal can turn into a superb one in a few years. All wines benefit from a few days' rest after being transported.

The most important requirement concerns temperature. Next is avoidance of direct sunlight, and lastly, cleanliness to avoid mold formation and odors.

Inspecting an aging red wine for the amount of sediment thrown along the bottle side. The horizontal position of the bottle is maintained.

THE TEMPERATURE of the storage area should be, ideally, between 55° and 60° F. An area where the temperature rises above 70° or falls below 45° is not advisable. The evenness of the temperature is very important. Violent changes are to be avoided.

Since the wine is to rest undisturbed, the location must be free from vibrations which could agitate the wine and prevent the slow deposit of sediment. The bottles are laid on their side, so that the wine covers the cork, keeping it wet and swollen. This way no air gets into the bottle. If the label is positioned at the top, the sediment will be readily visible.

SEDIMENT is thrown in the normal process of aging. It is a precipitate of solids and crystals and, particularly in red wines, a sign that the wine is aging properly. White wine often has a deposit, much less abundant, and usually in the form of tiny clear crystals. Neither kind of deposit is to be considered a defect. Cloudiness or continued lack of clarity are serious defects and may indicate a wine is not fit to be drunk.

SPACE LIMITATIONS allowing for storage of 24 bottles or less can be solved by the use of any number of wine racks, readily available in stores or from mail-order houses. Because of the small amount stored, it is not likely that any bottle will long remain. Pick the coolest convenient spot, away from any direct sunlight, vibrations or jolting disturbance. A more satisfactory solution, where space allows, is to use a closet, away from heating pipes or appliances. Strong, inch-thick shelving can be installed according to the suggested scheme shown in the diagram below.

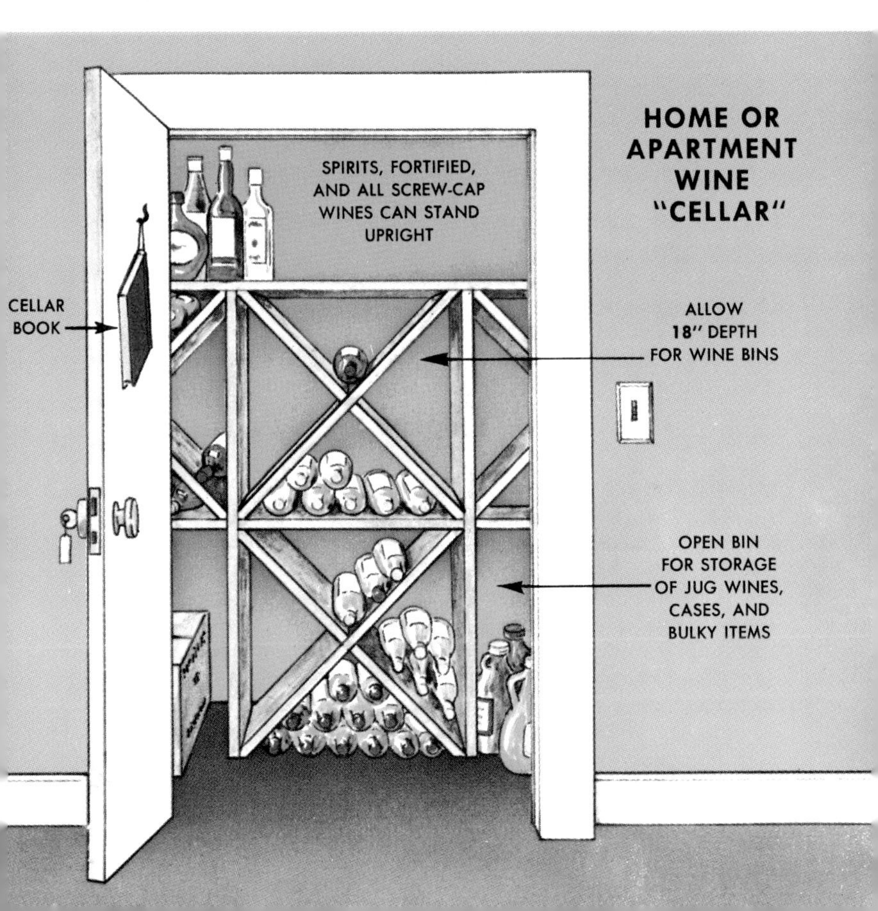

STORAGE RACKS AND BINS come in every size and shape, and in prices ranging from very reasonable to ridiculous. The author could not resist including his own design, shown on the opposite page, for a modular wine rack requiring only a little skill in carpentry, made of inexpensive plywood, and very flexible in space requirements. As many as 12 modular units, storing 72 bottles, can be stacked safely on top of each other.

THE BASE MODULE differs from the other modules, establishing the base for a vertical pile of tilted 6-bottle racks. The dimensions of the two sides, and the back piece are different. They are shown in the left bottom corner of the sketch. Note the different angles for the sides. The feet, indicated as 2″ x 2″ lumber, are optional, and can be made high enough to permit sweeping. One base module is needed for every stack. A stack of 8 modules, including the base, stands about five feet high and has proven most convenient. Higher stacks make the top racks hard to reach.

ALL THE OTHER MODULES are similar to each other and lock securely to each other and to the base module. The bottles are tilted toward the neck at a slight angle (10°), insuring a thoroughly wet and tight cork. The same effect is accomplished with the bottles completely horizontal—the angle helps to secure the stability of the structure.

Labels can be affixed to the face of the racks, identifying the wine clearly without the necessity of sliding the bottles out of the lower racks. Self-sticking labels or Dymo plastic strip labels have been found very effective.

The home craftsman, especially if a table saw is available, can make and assemble an 8-module rack in one day or less.

A good deal of time can be saved if similar pieces are all cut at the same time. The angles are more likely to fit perfectly if the same setting is used for making the cuts, rather than trying to match the setting at a later time.

The holes for the bottle necks are adequate for most bottles. They should not be made any smaller than 1½″ in diameter. The finished modules can be painted, stained and varnished or left raw. Attractively finished, they can be used as a room divider in a small apartment, providing that the heat and sunlight requirements are observed.

MODULAR WINE RACKS

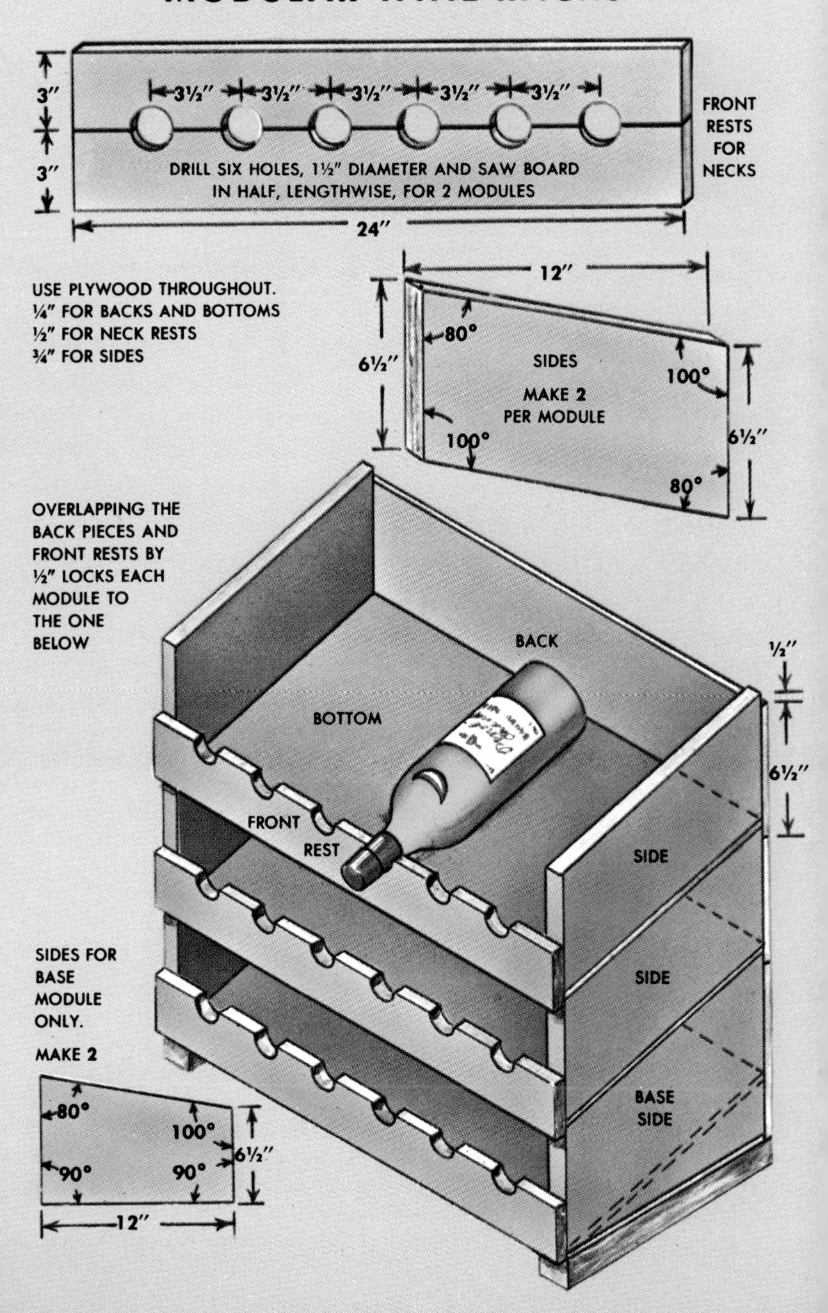

SERVING WINE

A lot of nonsensical "rules," ostentatious ritual, and meaningless procedures have, for too long, unnecessarily complicated the simple business of serving wine. Like any other food, certain commonsense procedures are followed for the convenience and enjoyment of those who are to partake of it. The considerate hosts serve the food in the usual order, each dish cool, cold, or hot, as its recipe requires, and in the type of plate, bowl, or cup best suited for it. A guest would have good reason to be concerned about the sanity of a host who took the temperature of the soup with a thermometer, and then proceeded to serve it in a saucer! There *are* wine thermometers on sale, probably next door to the shop selling thimble-sized colored stemware as "wine glasses." Let's throw out this foolishness and examine some more sensible alternatives:

TEMPERATURE. Most white wines taste better when cool. The degree of coolness, or cold, is completely a matter of personal preference. The delicate flavor and fragrance of a fine white wine can disappear if it is served too cold. A poorer white wine, having less to lose, can take more chilling than a finer vintage. The temperature can be determined by feel, either on the hand, or holding the bottle against the cheek.

Rosés, like whites, should be served cool, and the observations above apply to them.

Reds are supposed to be served "*at room temperature.*" This is a phrase which has confused many people, so let's look at what it really means. It originated in the days before central heating and air-conditioning, when wine cellars were really cold rooms below ground level, and dining rooms were heated by a fireplace.

A red wine should reach "room temperature" after being brought from a cooler cellar or storage closet by standing for an hour or two in a room where the temperature is between 70° and 80° F. The wine itself should *not* be 70°, much less 80°! *Never* try to speed the process by applying any heat. The wine will warm in the glass after a few moments. Here again, the temperature is a matter of personal preference.

OPENING THE BOTTLE. Red wines should be opened about one hour before serving. This enables the wine to come in contact with the air and release the complex fragrances of its bouquet. It is called "letting the wine breathe." The better the red wine, the more important this procedure becomes. White wines do not seem to need this long period of breathing and may be opened a few moments before serving.

Whenever possible, the wine should be opened at the table, providing a pleasurable anticipation for those who are to share it. The capsule can be torn off, or for those who enjoy the looks of a wine bottle, it may be cut carefully just below the bottle's lip. The cork is then wiped with a damp sponge or cloth to remove any mold or other matter which may have accumulated under the capsule and would be likely to impart a bad taste to the wine.

The cork is then extracted and, if necessary, the lip is wiped. Pulling the cork can be done with a flourish or in embarrassing, fumbling ignominy, depending on whether you have a good corkscrew or not. All the leverage devices on corkscrews are good and a great help in extracting the sometimes tenacious barrier between you and the wine. The same cannot be said about the "worm," the business end of the tool and the really important part. Too many corkscrews are really augers which bore a hole in the cork, weakening it or even tearing a gaping hole down the center.

A proper worm is a coiled spiral of steel wire, with the point *exactly in line* with the spiral, *not* centered on it. The open space in the middle of the spiral must be large enough to allow an ⅛″-wide paper match to be inserted. Finally the worm should be 2½″ long, the size of the longest corks.

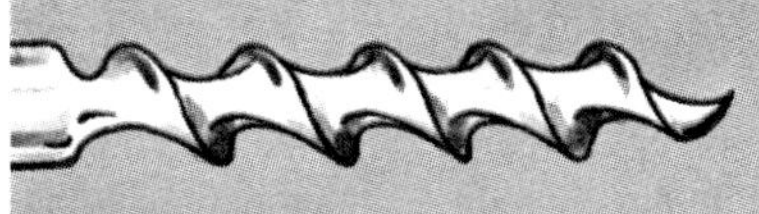

THIS DESIGN WILL BORE A HOLE IN THE CORK AND DOES NOT HOLD THE WEAKENED CORK FIRMLY.

PROPER WORM

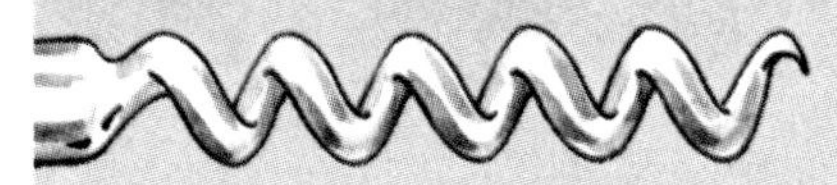

THE SPIRAL WILL FOLLOW THE POINT AND GIVE A FIRM GRIP ON THE CORK.

Having opened the bottle, the host will pour some wine into his glass, examine it without making a "production," sniff it, and taste it before he pours for his guests. This is a sensible and gracious tradition. His glass will catch any stray bits of cork present, and he will assure himself that the wine is fit to serve to his guests.

There is another "tradition," hopefully on its way to oblivion, of wrapping the bottle in a napkin, a pointless and silly affectation. All it does is to hide the label from the interested guest who is curious about the wine.

WINEGLASSES provide a field day in the exercise of foolishness and the exploitation of credulous innocents.

In the isolation of medieval times, every wine-growing region developed its own type of drinking vessel, and later its own design in wineglasses. The eye does play a part in our enjoyment of wine, and any wine worth drinking seems to taste better in a clear, crystalline long-stemmed glass than in a tin cup. But there is no need to have closets full of assorted glasses to match the types of wines served. The all-purpose wineglass, a graceful tulip-shaped bowl atop a well-proportioned stem, is adequate and satisfactory for serving all wines. It was pioneered by the late Harold Grossman and other sensible wine lovers and is now made by a number of glass manufacturers. The price is reasonable and it can be found in any good department store. If a little more variety is desired, two other glasses shown below are recommended. Wineglasses should be large enough to hold a four-ounce serving when half-full, and clear to appreciate the color.

You can use the thimble-sized wineglasses Aunt Mary gave you as a wedding present to serve cordials.

DECANTING is necessary when serving a red wine which, in the course of aging, has thrown a deposit of sediment on the side of the bottle. It is pointless to decant a clear wine. One with a very slight deposit may be poured directly by the exercise of care or with the help of a wine basket.

Decanting requires a funnel, a source of light, a decanter, and a steady hand. The latter determines the proportion of clear wine obtained before pouring has to stop.

The bottle to be decanted can be taken directly from the storage rack, gently so as not to disturb the sediment deposited on the side, and decanted. If time allows, it may be stood upright for a few days, allowing the deposit to slide gently down the side into the groove at the bottom. This usually insures a greater amount of clear wine to be extracted.

Decanting normally proceeds as outlined in the following five steps:

1. The entire capsule is removed so that the wine passing through the neck can be clearly seen.
2. The neck and cork are wiped clean of mold and other matter.
3. The cork is extracted.
4. A light source, a small flashlight or candle, is positioned so as to shine up through the neck of the bottle as the wine is poured through the funnel into the decanter.
5. At the first sign of sediment thread or particles swimming by in the illuminated portion of the neck, pouring stops. Careful, steady pouring should result in all but an ounce or two of muddy liquid being left in the bottle. Do not attempt to salvage the remains by further decanting or filtering. The wine in the decanter should be sparkling clear. The foolish ritual of smelling the cork is one we could all do without. Since the host has the first drink poured in his glass, he can tell from it whether the wine is "corky" or not.

THE WINETASTING PARTY

Over the past few years this pleasant and temperate form of entertainment has become increasingly popular. Its great flexibility adapts to any size crowd, any size place, and any size budget. The wine provides a conversation piece for even the shiest guest. New taste harmonies are discovered. The party provides a most pleasant way to learn more about wines. A few suggestions follow, only to point the way, for the variety of possibilities is almost infinite, limited only by the ingenuity of the host or hostess in both the wines that are served and the food that best sets off the wines.

THE NUMBER OF WINES to be served can vary from a minimum of four to a maximum of eight. Six wines have proven to be just about the most popular assortment that non-professionals can cope with. The idea is to taste, exchange impressions, and enjoy the wines.

THE AMOUNT OF WINE is, of course, directly related to the number of people at the party. For tasting purposes, a bottle of wine is generally estimated to serve from 12 to 18 persons. Each gets about two ounces of the wine, an amount sufficient to determine the characteristics and form an impression. This does not allow for seconds, but if six wines are presented, each guest will consume the equivalent of a half-bottle. This is a satisfying amount but not enough to impair faculties, especially when the wine is taken with adequate food.

THE CHOICE OF WINE to serve at a winetasting party is limited only by availability and budget. Even within the limitations of a very modest budget the themes and variations are almost unlimited. The wines can, for instance, be all reds, all whites, or a combination. They may be wines of one country or of several countries, or a varietal from several regions, or assorted vintage years of a single wine, or different wines of a given year, etc.

THE FOOD, like the wines, can be as simple or as elaborate as the hosts, or group, decide.

The usual, simplest, and least expensive is bread or crackers with assorted cheeses. Usually the milder cheeses which set off wine to best advantage without overpowering the more delicate ones are recommended: Swiss, Gouda, Muenster, Fontina, Brie, and

Camembert are among those easily obtainable.

Hot hors d'oeuvres, canapés, fresh fruit, and raw vegetables with dips are more elaborate accompaniments. Still more elaborate is a buffet chosen to accompany the selected wines. Each course of the buffet can have its own wine. Again, the hosts' imagination can range far and wide, remembering that the majority of wines are made to accompany food.

GLASSES, until recently, were a problem for the hosts of a home winetasting. Not everyone has a hoard of stemware to serve six or more wines to a score of guests. Renting glasses from a catering service is not always convenient or within the budgeted expense. The best solution has come in the form of the inexpensive, disposable, crystal-clear plastic 5-ounce "glass." It has been well received at the fanciest full-dress affairs as well as at the simplest.

A separate glass can be provided for each wine; rinsing bowls can be conveniently located if only one glass is used; or new glasses can be used when shifting from white to red wine, etc.

Crystal-clear plastic "glasses" are attractive and inexpensive.

If truly great wines are to be tasted, they deserve separate and fitting glassware which should be available to those who can afford to serve the grands crus.

A WINETASTING PARTY can be given at any time, but the weekend, from Friday night to Sunday afternoon, seems to be the preferred time. In good weather, facilities permitting, an outdoor setting can be perfect.

Usually, a winetasting of six wines lasts a little more than two hours. Guests should be advised to come on time, so that all can taste the same wine at the same time. Invitations should read: "Sunday afternoon, from 4 to 6 PM, *starting promptly at 4*."

Generally, it is a good idea to have the food at separate tables from the wine. This promotes free movement and mixing of the guests, and a freer exchange of conversation.

Small buckets should be provided for those who do not wish to finish the wine left in their glass.

Smoking prohibitions, as far as tasting wine is concerned, apply only to professionals who must keep their palates absolutely keen in order to detect faults in the wines they taste. They do not taste for enjoyment, as the partygoers do.

Here are some suggestions to help make your winetasting party a most enjoyable experience for both hosts and guests:

1. If possible, collect the wine a few days ahead of the party and *rest* it, standing upright.

2. Arrange the table or tables for the food and wine to allow free movement of the guests.

3. Cool the white wines and the rosés in time for serving at the desired temperature. Open the red wines about one hour before serving.

4. Plan the sequence of serving: whites before reds, and dry wines before the sweeter ones.

5. The pouring can be done by the hosts alone, for a small gathering, by helpers, or the guests can help themselves.

6. Provide material for making notes. Ruled index cards, 3″ x 5″, are fine for very brief notations; larger sizes may be unwieldly.

Avoid jargon, one of the many obnoxious attributes of the wine snob. It is far more agreeable, for most people, to share a pleasant experience than to put down a novice by fattening one's ego at his expense. The only thing fattened is an already adipose head.

It is, admittedly, difficult to describe the taste of wine and other foods, but it can be done in simple terms.

A. W. Laubengayer, first President of the American Wine Society, a consumer-oriented group, proposed a list which is a model for clear description of the attributes of wine:

To describe color: Clear, brilliant, hazy, cloudy, red, white, rose, pale green, greenish-yellow, nearly colorless, golden, amber, straw, pink, light red, ruby, tawny, brown.

To describe body, the feeling of substance in wine: Thin, light, full-bodied, heavy, viscous.

Here is a silly, ostentatious way of holding a stemmed wine glass. There is no scientific or sensible justification for this form of wine snobbery.

The stem is not only a support for the bowl, but provides a graceful and natural handle for holding the glass securely in any normal position.

To describe odor: Fragrant, grapy, flowery, delicate, fruity, spicy, sharp, acidic, vinegary, unpleasant, pungent, sulfurous, medicinal, musty, yeasty, earthy.
To describe taste: Dry, semi-dry, sweet, cloying, tart, sharp, fresh, nippy, refreshing, vinegary, sour, acidic, clean, bitter, fruity, mellow, soft, smooth, delicate, harsh, spritely, flat, bland, insipid, coarse, puckery, astringent, robust, yeasty, nutty, rank, earthy, musty, mousey, woody, resinous, medicinal, etc.

THE B.Y.O.B. PARTY. The initials stand for Bring Your Own Bottle, an increasingly popular and very economical arrangement.

A few compatible people gather in one home, or club room, each pair of guests bringing one bottle of wine to share and compare. The food is either provided by the host couple, or its cost divided by those attending. The type of wines should be decided in advance, when the party is planned.

Often these gatherings develop into very pleasant "tasting clubs." A good way to start a chain of parties of this kind is to have each guest bring his favorite wine. It helps to establish the taste direction of the group and provide a guide for following tastings.

THE BLIND TASTING, where the labels of the wines are masked, may be used for a variety of reasons. It adds the pleasurable element of a game

Set-up for Blind Wine Tasting.

to the party atmosphere, and it prevents "tasting the label," permitting the wine to be judged on its own merits. It can be used to grade the wines from least liked to best liked, and gradations between the two extremes.

As knowledge of the tasters increases, it can be used to identify the wines, or the grapes, and for real "pros" the vintage years of a single type of wine.

There are, again, infinite options for the use of blind tastings. When wines are to be identified by type it is usual to leave the bottle in a paper bag, tied under the neck to permit pouring but hiding the shape of the bottle.

After all have made their guesses, the bottles, or labels, are uncovered. Forbearance to crow over a right choice, or guess, is a virtue all the wrong guessers will appreciate. Remember that drinking wine is essentially fun, and its enjoyment may be diminished by taking the art of winetasting too seriously. As the kindly philosopher, Harry Golden, says: "Enjoy! Enjoy!".

WINING AND DINING OUT

Restaurants serving good food and good wine at reasonable prices are very rare. The number is slowly increasing, however, due largely to pressure from more knowledgeable consumers.

The markup on wine in a restaurant can double or triple the cost of the wine compared with its price in a retail store. Often the big markups are on wines bottled for restaurant use exclusively.

When restaurateurs finally realize that having wines at prices the average patron can afford will increase their revenue, we shall be able to have wine routinely with our meals without being victimized by ridiculously high prices.

A wine list should give a good range of choice, in keeping with the menu being offered. It should have a few high-quality wines, a larger number of good-quality wines in a moderate price range, and a few acceptable, honest carafe wines which can also be had by the glass. There should be a reasonable balance of imported and American vintages.

THE WINE LIST should be, but seldom is, brought to you together with the menu. Ask for it before you order anything. Scan both quickly to get a general idea of what is available. Then, when you and your guests have made your choices from the menu, the wine or wines can be selected.

If a red wine suits everyone's choice, look for American varietals, French Côtes du Rhône, Beaujolais, or minor Bordeaux Châteaux for your best buys.

If a white wine is desired, look again among the American varietals or generics, French Muscadets, Alsatian or German regionals, and Italian whites for the lower-priced good buys.

Seek names that you recognize for an indication of the price markup, as well as for the quality range of the wines offered. Ask the wine steward for advice, but don't feel obligated to follow it. A good wine steward will respond to your interest in his wines, a poor one

Playing the "cork game" with the wine waiter.

will try to push the wines with the biggest markup.

If the choice from the menu is mixed you can order two wines, in half-bottles or carafes if the latter are available. Do not be bullied into getting an expensive wine.

Once you have made your choice, order the wine immediately and give specific orders that it be served with the dish it accompanies.

WHEN THE WINE COMES, it should be presented to you *unopened* so you can verify that it is the one you ordered. Look for discrepancies in vintage year, name, or brand. You need not refuse it if a plausible explanation for any change is given and you are satisfied that an inferior wine has not been substituted. When you have verified that it is the one desired, the waiter will open it and pour you a small quantity for your approval. Look for a good clear color. If the wine is cloudy or hazy, refuse it. If the color is good, sniff for unpleasant smells. A corky or a sulfurous smell is cause for rejection. If the wine passes this test, taste it. If the taste is unpleasant, back it goes. Otherwise you can signal that it is acceptable and may be poured.

In some restaurants the wine steward will want to play "the cork game." He will hand you the cork and you are expected to sniff and examine it for signs of deterioration which may have affected the wine. This is a pointless ritual since you will taste the wine before accepting it. You can play the game if it amuses you.

When you refuse a wine, there should be no argument from either the wine steward or the captain. Usually, however, you will be satisfied with the wine, and in that case do not hesitate to tell the waiter, the wine steward, and the manager. Encourage the serving of good wines at reasonable prices.

WINE AND WEDDINGS

Wine has been closely associated with weddings from time immemorial—in the ritual of many cultures and religions and in the feast following the ceremony. In our Western culture the newlyweds are traditionally toasted in Champagne or a festive sparkling wine. Some Eastern countries, influenced by the West, have taken up this pleasant custom.

The Champagne and Champagne punches served at a wedding reception add gaiety to the occasion without adding to the financial burden on the father of the bride. Champagne can actually be less expensive than the equivalent in hard liquor. It can be served at a stand-up reception or at a sit-down dinner, and is always impressive and really festive.

GOOD CHAMPAGNE is available in a wide price range. The more expensive French Champagnes cost from twice to three times as much as American Champagnes. Vintage products cost a few dollars more than non-vintage ones. Bottle-fermented Champagne costs more than bulk-process wine. A non-vintage California or New York State Champagne is often the best buy. Sparkling wines produced by artificial carbonation are not recommended.

FOR CHAMPAGNE PUNCH it is not essential to use the highest-quality Champagne. It should be a good one but a lower-priced type can be used. The delicate flavor of the wine tends to be subdued in punch.

THE BRIDE is often given a number of showers, and with young people's growing interest in wine, a wine shower for the groom is becoming a welcome event in which the usually ignored male gets a place in the sun during the prenuptial festivities. The aim of the wine shower is to start the newlyweds with a wine cellar, even if it must reside in the coolest closet of their future home in a city apartment.

Obviously the first choice for a gift will be wine itself—a bottle, an assortment, or a case. If the couple-to-be have known preferences, that makes the choice easier; if not, the donor should be guided by his or her own preference.

There are many other choices, besides wines which make very suitable gifts for a wine shower: *Corkscrews,* plain or fancy, as long as they have a proper "worm," as described earlier (page 115); *cork extractors* of the air-pressure variety; all-purpose *wine glasses,* as described on page 116; *decanters; decanting funnels*—glass, plastic, or silver; and *bottle racks,* which come in every shape, material, and size imaginable.

Wine and wine cookery books are a welcome addition to the young wine lovers' bookshelves. See page 154.

The wine shower can be combined with an informal wine tasting, featuring some of the wines brought as gifts.

WINE AND FOOD

For most wines, a happy marriage with food is the ideal culmination of life, the destiny their makers intended. The occasion can be a royal feast, such as the matching of a *grand cru* with a masterpiece of *haute cuisine,* or it may be a joyous, unpretentious country wedding of an honest, sturdy vintage with a simple but tasty dish.

The matching of wine to food, like all taste preferences, is essentially a subjective operation. There are no *rules,* only *opinions*. The combinations generally accepted as "rules" are only the opinions of many epicures, gourmets, and others, not necessarily a majority, and in any case cannot be binding on anyone. There is no *right* or *wrong* choice. Just as beauty is in the eye of the beholder, a satisfying combination of tastes lies in the taste buds of the taster.

Variations from the consensus are not *mistakes* but simply reflect a more or less unorthodox taste. It would be presumptuous to condemn an unorthodox choice or denigrate the taste of the person making it.

On the following pages are suggestions for wine-food combinations. The listings start with the most generally accepted matchings and proceed through other possibilities to the more unusual combinations. The types of wines may be listed in broad categories, such as "Claret," which then stands for most clarets, from Château-bottled Classified Growths to Claret-type jug wine. The wine chosen within that broad range may depend on price, availability, or, more to the point, the selector's taste preference.

All the photographs of food in this section are by courtesy of the California Wine Institute.

APPETIZERS, often served as a stand-up prelude to a meal, allow for the greatest variety of wines to be served with the goodies. *Champagne* or other sparkling wines, and rosés will usually serve for any combination. Dry *Sherries* are also an all-purpose appetizer accompaniment. One wine may be served or several, but more than three can be considered a bit ostentatious unless the event is a sort of mini-wine tasting. Let the degree of flavor in the food determire the wine; serve subtle, delicate wines with mild-flavored food, bigger wines with the stronger-flavored foods.

Cheeses: Most wines go well with most cheeses, but again the degree of flavor should determine the choice of wine. The stronger cheeses such as aged Cheddar, Stilton, and Roquefort call for the big red *Burgundies, Barolo* and *Clarets,* the bigger dry *Sherries* and *Madeiras.* With milder cheeses such as Brie, Swiss, and Muenster, serve lighter reds like *Beaujolais,* light *Clarets,* light dry *Sherries,* and *Loire, Provence,* and *New York State reds.*

Dry and even semi-dry white wines are very suitable with most cheeses. *Pinot Chardonnay, Pinot Blanc, Mosels, Gewürztraminers,* and *Chilean Chablis* are but a few suggestions to accompany these.

Caviar: Dry *Sherry, Chablis, Champagne, sparkling rosé.*

Smoked Salmon: Dry *Sherry,* dry *Madeira, Champagne,* and other *sparkling wines.*

Oysters and **Shellfish:** *Chablis, Pinot Blanc, Pinot Chardonnay,* dry *Graves,* dry *Sherry, Green Hungarian.*

SOUPS vary in texture as well as taste, from clear consommé to thick and hearty minestrone, and some are served cold, others hot. The menu can be planned so that the same wine is served throughout the meal, beginning at the soup course. The same rule of thumb holds here: hearty wines with hearty soups, delicate wines with the more subtly flavored soups.

Cream Soups, such as bisques, milk or cream chowders or creamed vegetables are enhanced by dry white wines such as *Pouilly-Fuissé, Chenin Blanc, Alsatians, Mosels.* Or serve semi-dry whites such as *Pineau de la Loire, Graves, Rheingaus, Soave,* and the all-purpose *rosés. New York State, Ohio* and *Canadian whites* are a bit sweeter but well suited to the delicate soups.

Turtle Soup and black bean soup are enhanced by adding a tablespoon of medium *Sherry* to each plateful. The same *Sherry* can, of course, be served to the guests.

Hearty Soups such as Beef and Vegetable, Oxtail, etc., are very good with whatever red wine is to follow. *Zinfandel, Chianti, Beaujolais, Nebbiolo,* and *Spanish reds* are all among the suitable wines and add a savory touch to all hearty soups.

SIMPLE DISHES, good in themselves become even better when served with a nice, simple wine. The American jug wines are the best answer to what wine to serve with such popular staple dishes as hamburgers, hot dogs, baked beans, Spam and other luncheon meats, toasted cheese sandwiches, hash, etc.

The next best choice is the inexpensive good wines of Spain, Italy, Portugal, Australia, Chile, Germany, and France. However, it has become increasingly difficult to find inexpensive good wines from Germany and France, although some are still available.

Hamburger, meat loaf, meat patties and the like are enhanced by such wines as California *Zinfandel*, Gallo's *Hearty Burgundy* and *Paisano*, Christian Brothers' *Burgundy*, and *New York State reds*.

Hot Dogs, luncheon meats, cold cuts, and other spiced or preserved meats are usually best with dry white wines.

There are any number of California and New York State *Chablis*-type jug wines which, though they bear little or no resemblance to true Chablis, are good companions for spiced meats. Other choices include *Rhine*-type American and Chilean wines.

Cheese sandwiches, rarebits, etc., are good with either red, white, or rosé jug wines. The degree of dryness is the drinker's choice.

Hash, and variations on that theme, seem suited to rosés and reds, the rosés preferably on the dry side.

Salads made with vinegar are incompatible with *any* wine. Those made without vinegar are often good with the all-purpose rosés, or with light whites which can range from dry to reasonably sweet, again depending on the diner's personal preference.

If you are an adult addicted to peanut butter sandwiches, try a glass of *Zinfandel* with them.

BEEF is universally considered best served with red wine. If the meat is roasted or broiled, the range of choice is very wide, starting with *Clarets,* through the bigger *Burgundies,* progressing through the hearty *Chiantis* and robust *Barolos,* to the big dark *Spanish* and *Hungarian reds.*

If wine is used in cooking the meat, or in the preparation of its sauce, the same wine should be served with the beef.

In American reds, *California's varietals* offer a wide range of taste and degrees of bigness. *New York State reds* are lighter. The *French reds,* besides those named above, can include those of the *Jura* and *Loire,* both lighter and less expensive. Also on the lighter side are the Italian *Valpolicellas,* the Portuguese *Vinho Verdes,* and the Spanish *Riojas.*

The quality of the wine should be matched to the quality of the meat—a noble roast with a *grand cru,* minute steak with jug red.

LAMB, being a lighter red meat than beef, calls for relatively lighter red wines that will not overpower the delicate flavor of the meat but enhance it. Fine red *Bordeaux* and aged California *Cabernets* are generally considered top choices for roasted or broiled fine cuts. The following red wines are also eminently suitable: *Beaujolais, Loire, Jura,* the lighter *Côtes du Rhône,* American varietals such as *Gamay,* light *Pinot Noir,* and *Baco.* Light *Italian* and *Portuguese reds* can be very good with lamb.

Here again, if a red wine has been used in the cooking, it should be the choice for serving with the dish.

The all-purpose rosé may also be used, providing it is not too sweet. While whites are not the usual choice, some of the bigger Alsatian wines can be excellent with lamb, particularly if it is cooked with the same white wine. The Germans serve their drier whites with lamb dishes.

VEAL tastes best with wines that will not overpower its delicate flavor. The lighter wines, whites, rosés, and some reds are the best choices. The light reds are indicated when the veal is made with a tasty sauce, the whites and rosés when roasted.

Many of the American white varietals can be used with great success. The big white *Burgundies* of France are often too much of a good thing for veal. The lightest red *Bordeaux, Beaujolais,* and American red varietals, particularly the *New York reds,* are favored by many for veal, particularly when it is served with a wine sauce, as in the case of Veal Scallopini or Veal Marsala. In the latter case, the *Marsala* wine is not routinely served, contrary to the usual rule of thumb of serving the wine used in preparing it.

FRESH PORK, can be treated much like veal.

The white wines can be a little bigger, and most people in the United States seem to prefer a not too dry white with roast pork. Rosés are usually excellent with fresh pork, and the degree of dryness is once again a matter of personal preference. The dry *Tavels* and the *Provence* rosés have a nice "edge" of acidity which cuts the fattiness of pork.

The reds, even the lightest ones, do not seem to be the favorite or even popular choice to go with fresh pork. A possible exception could be made in the case of the lightest Portuguese *Vinho Verdes.* However, there is no *rule,* as such, and if you like a red with pork, enjoy it!

Sparkling wines, if not too sweet, can be quite suitable.

HAM, especially baked with a sweet glazing, is one of the problem dishes to match with a wine. White wines and rosés can provide a suitable accompaniment. Both whites and rosés are usually preferred not too dry. Many wine drinkers will admit that fresh or hard cider or beer taste better with ham than many available wines.

Generally, light fresh wines, not too dry but with a bit of tartness, can be quite agreeable with ham. The clean, refreshing taste cuts across the pronounced taste of the ham; likewise, the smoky or salty ham taste provides a counterpoint of flavor to the wine.

FOWL comes in such a variety of species and is prepared in so many ways that each type of dish must be treated separately.

CHICKEN, roasted, is usually served with light white wine or rosé. It can be served with bigger wines, including the white *Burgundies,* as well as the fragrant wines of the *Rheingau* and *Mosel,* the more robust *Alsatians,* the California *Gewürztraminers, Pinot Chardonnays,* and the delicate *New York State white varietals.* The same wines can be served if the dish comes with a light and delicate sauce. Reds can be used with the stronger sauces such as those used in Chicken Cacciatore. In that case, serve the lighter red *Bordeaux, American red varietals,* and the more delicate *Italian reds.*

TURKEY has a stronger flavor than chicken, so the fuller white wines and the light reds suggested for chicken in the preceding paragraph can be used.

GOOSE, with still more flavor, is often served with light and medium red wines, and even with some of the bigger red wines, depending on the manner of preparation and the flavor of the sauce with which it is served.

DUCK and **GUINEA HEN** are all dark meat with a pronounced, distinct flavor. They can stand the big white wines and medium to big red ones.

The sauce and method of cooking determine the bigness of the wine to be served with either. The more pronounced the flavor of the sauce, the bigger can be the flavor and body of the wine served with the fowl.

Champagne, like rosé, is an all-purpose wine which can be served with all varieties of fowl.

SEAFOOD has a remarkable affinity for one wine above all others, the true Burgundian *Chablis.*

However there are a multitude of other white wines, and some reds too, which can enhance the enjoyment of a seafood dish. With grilled, poached, and mildly seasoned fish, the following whites are suggested: dry *Graves, Meursault, Muscadet, Alsatians,* dry *Rheingaus* and *Mosels, Soave, Verdicchio,* American varietals such as *Pinot Blanc, Chardonnay, Chenin Blanc, Delaware,* and the dry white generics such as *Chablis* and *Rhine* types.

Fish with spicy or pungent sauces, like other foods, calls for more flavor in the wine that accompanies it. Here the choice broadens with the addition of *Gewürztraminer,* the *Hungarian dry whites,* the bigger *white Burgundies,* and white *Hermitage.*

The famed *Bouillabaisse* of Marseille, a wonderfully pungent fish stew, is traditionally accompanied by the dry white wine of *Cassis,* a little fishing village east of Marseille. There are infinite variations of the recipe, allowing for an equal number of variations in the wine to be served. The more flavorful dry whites are best. The Italian variation, *Zuppa di Pesce,* marries well with the dry Italian whites and their American equivalents.

Cioppino, a superb San Francisco specialty, probably imported by Italian fishermen, has a distinctive pungent combination of tomatoes, garlic, basil, and oregano added to the fish and other seafood. It is cooked in hearty red wine, and none but a big robust red can be served with it and survive the heady taste. The more assertive California red varietals are natural companions for cioppino such as *Petite Sirah, Barbera,* and *Zinfandel.*

Paella, a succulent Spanish dish whose ingredients vary from cook to cook, is basically a combination of seafood and sausages cooked with saffron rice. A feast for the eye and the palate, it has a rich taste calling for big wines, either reds or whites depending on the basic ingredients. The Spanish whites and reds of Rioja and of Valdepeñas are obviously the first choice, but almost any big dry white, such as *Pinot Chardonnay,* and the multitude of robust reds from any wine country are suitable.

GAME, whether feathered or furred, is considered at its best with a red wine. A brace of pheasants or a haunch of venison is, for most of us, an unusual event, a special and festive occasion. It calls for some of the best dry reds in our cellars, a choice among the well-**aged *Bordeaux or California*** *Cabernets* of great vintage, our great *Côtes du Rhône* such as *Hermitage* or *Châteauneuf-du-Pape*, great Burgundies from the *Côte de Nuits* or *Côte de Beaune*, or an old Italian *Barolo* or *Gattinara*.

On a more modest scale, lesser growths of the above-named regions make a very fine accompaniment to the spoils of the chase. There are many fine dry red Burgundies outside the aristocratic vineyards and their equivalents in the **Côtes du Rhône**. They include California varietals and some generics, and for those who may want a bit less dryness, some of the reds now produced in New York State. Here, too, be guided by the rule of thumb that the stronger the taste and flavor of the dish, the bigger must be the flavor and taste of the wine if it is not to be overpowered. A nice balance is always the aim.

Some game bird recipes use white wine in the preparation, and in such cases a sturdy white or *Champagne* is often the best choice for the wine to be served. The Germans usually serve their fine white wines, not always very dry, to very good advantage with wild game of all kinds. They have no native reds which can compare in quality with their superb whites.

SALADS in conjunction with wine require one major caution: If vinegar is used in the dressing, no wine is to be served with it. Vinegar kills the pleasant taste of *any* wine. That is why, in wine-drinking countries, a tossed salad is served last in a meal. American cuisine has, however, a great richness in salads that do not have vinegar, and wine can certainly be served with these to good advantage, since an elaborate salad is often the principal dish of a summer luncheon.

Whites are usually a better match for these salads than reds. Rosés are also very suitable, as well as *Champagne* or other sparkling wines, excluding Sparkling Burgundy. In some rare cases, such as a salad whose ingredient is beef, Sparkling Burgundy or light reds may be very good choices.

The variety of taste and texture in American salads is so great that the choice of wine to serve with them is almost infinite. It really boils down to the personal preference of the host or hostess with regard to the degree of dryness or lack of it in the wine chosen. The following paragraphs contain some general guidelines which may prove helpful.

The drier whites are considered better where the dressing is mainly mayonnaise. Dry rosés are also quite suitable.

Where cottage cheese is a major ingredient, the range is a bit broader, and can well include semi-dry and slightly sweet white wines and rosés.

Spicy or very pungent salads may be able to stand up to a red wine, usually on the light side, such as the New York reds made from the native grape.

Salads containing a preponderance of fruits call for the whites, ranging from dry to semi-dry, and even in some cases to whites and rosés which are quite sweet.

The fragrance of American white wines made from the native grape is usually well suited to the American salad repertoire, even though it is unlikely that the creators of the recipes had wine in mind as an accompaniment. It is a truism that for the best combinations of food and wine one should look first to the wines of the country where the recipe originates.

DESSERTS bring in all the sweet fortified wines for consideration. In some cases, the wine is the major part of the dessert, as when *Château d'Yquem,* a great *Tokay,* or *Trockenbeerenauslese* is served. All that is needed with these great wines are a few good cookies and you have a dessert fit for a king.

In a slightly less exalted category we can place *Port, Cream Sherry, Madeira, Málaga, Aleatico d'Elba, Malvasia,* and *Angelica,* to name but a few of the dessert wines which need little support to be the main dessert. They can, of course, be served with more elaborate pastries, creams, mousses and other delightful and pound-adding delicacies.

True *Sauternes* is sweet. It is really a contradiction of terms to label a wine *dry* Sauternes. With its cousin *Barsac,* this sweet wine is a dessert wine par excellence.

The sweeter German *Rheingau* wines are superb dessert wines. The sweet *Anjou* whites, the *Muscat de Frontignan,* the Greek *Samos,* and the Tuscan *Vin Santo* are also excellent dessert wines.

In American wines we can look to the sweet fortified wines of the port and sherry types, some very good *Muscatels, Angelicas,* and the American *Muscat de Frontignan.* Muscatel and Angelica have been maligned as cheap "wino" types, due to some inferior mass production aimed at exploiting the pitiful alcoholics. There are excellent California types made by the top vintners there.

CHEESE and wine have such a natural affinity for each other that almost any cheese and wine combination, within reason, will be tasty and enjoyable. A variety of cheeses usually accompanies a wine-tasting party. A piece of cheese, good hearty fresh bread, and a glass of wine are a favorite snack all around the wine-drinking world. When matching wine to cheese it must be remembered, for best results, that there are strongly flavored cheeses as well as medium and delicate ones. The combination should strive for balance, each complementing, and neither overpowering the other.

The above holds true of cheese dishes, and a good guide in choosing wine for them, is to think of their country of origin. The Swiss Fondue is enhanced by the dry white Swiss wines. Good alternate choices are the dry white California varietals, and less dry New York whites. The Alsatian quiche calls for any of the Alsatian whites, or the other wines of the French and German Moselle. The fine Luxembourg wines, where available, are an excellent alternate choice. The same type of wines served with quiche may also be used with any cheese soufflé.

Italian cheese dishes often have tomato among the lively ingredients, and this makes a red wine the first choice. The gamut runs from the light *Valpolicella* to the majestic *Barolo.* Sturdy reds from Spain, California, and the French Midi are also good companions for these hearty dishes.

Russian Cheese Blintzes may have been accompanied by vodka originally, but the light and fragrant white wines of the Rhine and Moselle are more suited to their delicate taste. Slightly sweet or semi-dry white wines also make a fine match.

FRUIT, like cheese, goes well with almost any wine, including a number of fortified ones, such as *Sherry* and *Port*.

Citrus fruits, like oranges and tangerines, are often preferred with light, semi-sweet or sweet white wines as well as with the fortified dessert wines. No wine seems to be good with grapefruit.

Apples and pears are good with any wine that has been served with the meal, and with dessert or fortified wines.

Strawberries are particularly suited to red wine, but rosés and dry or sweet whites are also very pleasant with this fragrant fruit.

Sliced fruit, served as a salad-dessert at the end of a meal, is delicious with the addition of almost any wine if fruit and wine are allowed to stand together for about a half hour before being served. A little powdered sugar may be added if desired, or if the fruit is a bit more tart than sweet. Sliced oranges with a rum dressing are a good match for the best of the sweeter Sherries as well as the not too dry Ports, Madeiras, and Málagas.

Champagne and rosé wines, two of the universal common denominators for just about any food, are also good companions for many fruits and fresh fruit dishes, either served as dessert, or during the day, between meals. These two wines are rarely out of place and almost never clash with the taste of fruit except with those of overpowering flavor.

NUTS and fortified wines are natural companions. English writers have rhapsodized at length on the classic combination of walnuts and fine *Port*. Their praise is well deserved, for the two produce through a subtle and complex chemistry of taste a perfect complement for each other.

While many red table wines are suitable, fortified wines are best suited to serving with nuts.

Dry Sherry, a superb apéritif wine, is a good choice before the meal. *Cream Sherry* goes well with dessert.

Madeira ranges from very dry to very sweet, with all gradations in between. Serve the dry ones with appetizers, the sweet ones with dessert.

Sicilian Malvasia and *Aleatico d'Elba* are sweet, dark dessert wines well suited to nuts and nutty cookies and desserts. They are particularly well suited to the crisp almond confections, a specialty of Italian shops.

WINE PUNCHES are easy to **make, convenient to serve, and** quite inexpensive. Even *Champagne Punch* can be relatively inexpensive for the festive occasion. The lower priced sparkling wines are indicated where they will be mixed with other wines and ingredients.

There are many recipes for all kinds of wine punches, some dry, many slightly sweet. Every wine cookbook usually has a section describing wine punches, and wine stores have booklets from many wine companies giving excellent recipes which can be had for the asking.

Sangria, the famous Spanish refresher, now comes ready-mixed in bottles. Home-made Sangria, from any of the dozens of readily available recipes, is better and considerably cheaper. The less expensive Spanish reds, as well as California and New York State reds, are a base for this fine summer drink.

The perfume of the native American grape in some of the New York State reds adds a pleasant taste variation to home-made Sangria. A dash of inexpensive brandy is suggested in some recipes. Wine punches can be made with just about any kind of wines—still wines, sparkling wines, Sherries and Ports, as well as some of the appetizer wines. They are particularly suited for serving in hot weather, at patio parties and the like, but are very welcome at all other times where a refreshing beverage is suitable to the occasion.

The simplest Summer drink is *Wine and Soda*—ice, wine, and soda in a tall glass. The wine may be red, white, or rosé.

BUFFETS are often a serve-yourself occasion, and the self-service can apply to the wines presented with the food. To make the operation smoother the wine or wines may be placed at a table standing apart from the food. It is rather difficult to juggle the plate, silver, etc., and balance a glass of wine at the same time. The wine should be picked up on a second trip or the host should go around to his guests and serve them.

Wines which require careful pouring should not be used or should have been decanted previously. The handling of wine bottles on a self-service buffet will stir up any sediment by the time the third guest pours his own portion. It is a wise host who will serve clear, unsedimented wines or decanted ones at such an occasion.

Many American wines are carefully clarified, and some are so thoroughly clarified that they lose much of their character in the process for the sake of clarity and brilliant color. White wines should be cooled previous to setting out at a buffet, and the ice bucket avoided in a self-service situation. It can become rather messy, but if the wines are served promptly there is no need of continuous chilling.

PICNICS are enlivened by wines, like any other occasion. The everyday wines are the best choice for a picnic meal as they are least likely to be hurt by the inevitable jostling.

Wines that can be transported without harm to their clarity and flavor should be chosen. The reds must be free of sediment that would be shaken up and lack time to settle before serving. Most American generics and white varietals are probably the best choice.

A previously prepared wine punch like Sangria makes an excellent picnic beverage. The soda water can be added at the time of serving, as well as the additional ice.

The wine or punch can be carried in a cooler or can be cooled on the spot in a convenient brook or stream, unless enough ice has been brought along for the purpose.

Unless the bottles have a twist cap closure, don't forget to bring a corkscrew! We have not been a wine-drinking country long enough to carry corkscrews routinely as the Europeans do.

WINERIES AND MUSEUMS

Vacationers on trips through the United States and abroad have found the wine regions among the most hospitable anywhere. Vintners make a product that enhances fellowship and gaiety. As a group they are about the most affable people in the world, glad to show their vineyards and wineries to interested visitors. They are craftsmen and artists in their chosen field, and proud of their work. A visit to a vintner, as the *Guide Michelin* puts it, "is well worth the detour."

Most wine regions have put together exhibits and memorabilia of tools, implements, equipment, and art work related to wine. Sometimes the collections include some beautiful antique glassware and drinking vessels. Most of these museums are supported by the local wine industry and there is no admission charge.

AMERICAN WINERIES almost without exception welcome visitors throughout the year. Many have regular tours, all ending most agreeably with a tasting of the wines. Information about the tours is readily available in the locality. Some out-of-the-way vineyards may require an appointment. California and New York State vintners have welcomed thousands upon thousands of visitors and tourists, and are extremely well organized in providing interestingly instructive tours and tastings.

ABROAD the arrangements may vary from country to country but the same affability is there, most vintners being delighted to show tourists their installations, whether modernized or awesomely ancient and traditional. There, too, the tour ends with a taste of the wine.

There is almost never any attempt to sell the visitor any wine, either in America or abroad. The vintner hopes you will remember his wine when you are shopping at home.

The Greyton H. Taylor Wine Museum in Hammondsport, New York.

THE GREYTON H. TAYLOR WINE MUSEUM housed the original Taylor Wine Company from 1883 to 1920. The exhibits range from 19th-century Champagne making and Prohibition era items to presses and "antique" equipment. There is also an extensive wine and viticulture library and a unique "Grape Library" of over 200 living individual grape varieties from all over the world. This museum is just north of Hammondsport, N.Y., in the middle of vineyards overlooking Keuka Lake. It is open from May 1 to October 31.

Nineteenth-century vat and hand wine pump at the Greyton H. Taylor Wine Museum are still operative.

EUROPE abounds in museums of every sort, and the wine centers all have some collections of artifacts related to the wines made in the region.

BEAUNE, the capital of Burgundian wine, has, in addition to the famous Hospices de Beaune, a fine Burgundian wine museum showing traditional equipment and methods of viticulture typical of this great wine region.

SIENA, one of the lovely cities of Italy's Tuscan region, has a unique "wine library," the *Enoteca Italica Permanente*, where the finest wines of Italy are displayed on shelves divided into the various wine regions of the country.

All the wines may be tasted, in several tasting rooms or in charming terrace gardens shaded by grape arbors. There is also a restaurant attached to the *Enoteca* where gastronomic specialties may be sampled along with the wines.

SPAIN'S Villafranca, the capital of the Panadés wine region, has a Wine Museum located in the ancient palace of the kings of Aragon. The impressive structure, built in 1285, houses exhibits portraying the history of Spanish viticulture.

In the center of the Sherry region, in Jerez de la Frontera, is the recently restored Palace of Wine, the headquarters of the Sherry producers. A charming, traditional Spanish setting houses a variety of exhibits related to the making and the enjoyment of Sherry. The tourist can obtain there all the information he needs to visit the neighboring *bodegas* where the famous wine is made.

THE WINE MUSEUM OF SAN FRANCISCO is the most recent addition to wine memorials. The rich and fascinating displays of this splendid institution justify the phrase following its name: "In Celebration of Wine and Life." The museum is sponsored by The Christian Brothers, who started collecting rare books, sculpture, glassware prints, and other artifacts on the subject of wine in the late 1930's.

The collecting started modestly enough but soon began to assume such proportions that a museum was decided upon. While the collection was still growing and being exhibited at major American and Canadian art museums, the building began to go up at the corner of Beach and Hyde Streets on San Francisco's picturesque historic waterfront. A Ceremonial Court provides a setting for wine-related activities.

A Young Bacchant, bronze by Jean Baptiste Carpeaux.

Noted artists represented in the collection of wine memorabilia include Altsdorfer, de Valdes, Baldung, Brebiette, Renoir, Chagall, Maillol, Picasso and Rouault. The collection is probably the single most important and inclusive assemblage in the U.S. of artistic expressions of grape vintage and wine making.

St. Geneviève of Paris as Patroness of the Wine Growers, carved lindenwood, polychromed originally. (French, about 1460)

Among the countries represented by the artistic pieces on display in the permanent collection are Austria, England, France, Germany, Italy, Spain, and the United States. The spacious exhibit halls cover more than five thousand square feet of floor space, excluding the Ceremonial Court, where additional exhibits may be displayed.

The famous Franz Sichel glass collection has been added to the museum's hoard of rare treasures. In addition to the beautiful glass pieces, it includes ancient and unusual drinking vessels and cups, some dating back to the Roman Empire of 1 B.C. The collection also includes exquisitely crafted crystal from later periods.

Bacchus as a Boy, parcel-gilt and patinated bronze statuette on oval base. (French, 18th century)

Wine museums are often located in or near the center of a wine region and afford the visitor an excellent opportunity to compare the old and the new in equipment, methods, and other artifacts of the region's wine making.

Even the most traditionally oriented wine making regions have seen dramatic changes in both equipment and techniques. The exhibits, in some places going back as much as a thousand years, reflect centuries of unchanging methods and picturesque but primitive equipment and tools which did little to lighten the vignerons' tasks.

The spectacular changes have come to the art and science of wine making quite recently. They perhaps lack the quaint esthetic attractiveness of the ancient artifacts, but they are bringing great benefits to the consumer.

For sheer beauty, the exhibits related to wine enjoyment are unmatched. Ancient civilizations and more recent elegant ages produced drinking vessels whose beauty speaks eloquently of their attitude toward the beverage they were designed to hold. The magnificent glassware of inspired design was obviously intended for a superbly delightful beverage more ambrosial than water.

Five Children as Vintagers, Meissen porcelain, about 1790.

MISCELLANY

THE AMOUNT OF WINE produced by the leading wine countries varies from year to year. Some countries are increasing the amount of wine produced year by year; others, show decreasing output. The table below shows a composite average of several years' production.

PROPORTIONATE WINE PRODUCTION

STABILIZED AT ABOUT 1,900,000,000 GALS. **ITALY**

STABILIZED AT ABOUT 1,750,000,000 GALS. **FRANCE**

SPAIN (STABLE)

ARGENTINA (STABLE)

U.S.S.R. (INCREASING)

PORTUGAL (STABLE)

UNITED STATES (INCREASING)

ALGERIA (DECREASING SIGNIFICANTLY)

W. GERMANY (SLIGHTLY DECREASING)

THE SHAPE OF A WINE BOTTLE is usually an indication of the *type* of wine it contains. Each was developed in the region of origin, but the most popular shapes, the sharp-shouldered Claret bottle, the sloping Burgundian, etc., were adopted by other wine regions. Note that German wines are differentiated by the color of the glass.

THE QUANTITY held in wine bottles is becoming more rigidly standardized. The table below shows the normal number of servings the standard bottles hold. Note that the servings for a wine tasting vary, depending on whether a 1-ounce serving is deemed sufficient or a more generous 2 ounces.

BOTTLE SIZE	CONTENT IN OUNCES	NUMBER OF SERVINGS			
		DINNER WINE	CHAMPAGNE	APPETIZER OR DESSERT WINE	FOR A WINE TASTING
SPLIT (⅖ Pt.)	6.4	1-2	1-2	2-3	3-5
TENTH (⅘ Pt.)	12.8	3-4	3-4	4-6	6-10
PINT	16	4-5	4-5	6-8	8-15
FIFTH (⅘ Qt.)	25.6	6-8	8	10-12	12-20
QUART	32	8-10	8-10	10-14	16-30
MAGNUM	52	16	16	—	25-50
½ GALLON	64	16-20	—	20-30	30-60
JEROBOAM	104	—	32	—	50
GALLON	128	30-40	—	40-60	60-100
REHOBOAM	156	—	48	—	70

KEEPING A RECORD of the wines in your cellar is enjoyable as well as useful. Any small notebook or set of file cards will do. The illustration shows a suggested form: a looseleaf folder, large enough to attach a label at the top, with room for comments below. Suggested notations: date purchased; store; price; quantity; date tasted; evaluation of color, odor, and taste. Be as specific and complete as you wish, including the food served.

A cellar book such as the one described is useful for guiding your shopping expeditions, recognition of labels, gloating over good finds, and avoiding bad ones.

Every occupation creates its own vocabulary to express its peculiar interests, procedures, and concerns. Vintners and those interested in wine, professionals and laymen, have created a language of wine. Some of it is clear, logical, and reasonable; some of it borders on jargon; and some is out-and-out jargon. The latter, unintelligible to most people, seems to serve only to boost the ego of the user, confuse the listener, and possibly detract from his enjoyment of the wine under discussion. This characteristic form of wine snobbery is being continually exposed and is, hopefully, on the way to the oblivion it richly deserves.

Describing taste, odor, and other sensory perceptions associated with wine, or food, is a difficult process at best. Without points of reference or familiar comparisons, there is need for a word or words with specific meaning as applied to sensory perceptions. Imagine describing the taste of an apple to an Eskimo.

On the pages following you will find a short glossary of terms often used in describing and discussing wine. Some are foreign words for which there are no equivalent words in English, and some are English words, such as *body, balance,* and *dry,* which have a special meaning when applied to the subject or wine.

The glossary is by no means complete since this little book has no pretentions of being an encyclopedia but is rather a primer on wines.

A number of readers will visit vineyards in their travels, and it may be wise to caution them against the use of at least two words which are anathema to most American vintners. Do not call American or Canadian wines "domestic" or refer to their winemaking process as "manufacturing." The derogatory implications in each are obvious. You will not endear yourself to your hosts or be considered an appreciative guest if you use these taboo words.

GLOSSARY

Acidity The agreeable sharp taste caused by natural fruit acids. In moderate amount it is a favorable characteristic, and is not to be confused with sourness, dryness, or astringency.

Aroma The fragrance of fresh fruit directly related to the variety of grape used to make the wine.

Astringency A normal characteristic of some young wines, usually caused by an excess of tannin, lessening with age. It has a puckering effect on the mouth.

Auslese German term for wine made from especially well-ripened and perfect bunches, including those affected with *Edelfaule*, or "noble rot."

Balance A term of high praise denoting a wine whose sugar content, acidity, and the many odor and taste elements are present in such proportions as to produce a harmonious and pleasant sensation.

Beerenauslese German name for the sweet, expensive wine made from individually picked berries affected with *Edelfaule*.

Body The taste sensation of substance in a wine, not necessarily related to alcoholic content. Opposite of thin.

Bouquet French word for the complex of odors given off by a mature wine when it is opened.

Brut French term designating driest (least sweet) grade of Champagne or sparkling wine of a particular vintner.

Cabinet or **Kabinett** German wine designation of a superior grade or special reserve.

Château A wine estate, particularly in Bordeaux region.

Clos A walled, or once-walled vineyard, mainly in Burgundy.

Cru Usually denotes high quality vineyard.

Dessert Wines Sweet or partially sweet still wines containing about 17 to 20% alcohol by volume.

Dinner Wines Still wines with a maximum of 14% alcohol by volume. Most, but not all, dinner wines are dry.

Domaine A wine estate.

Dry This much-abused word means nothing more than lacking in sweetness. The degree of dryness is determined by the proportion of total grape sugar converted to alcohol.

Edelfaule German for "noble rot," caused by a mold, *Botrytis cinera*, forming on overripe white grapes.

Estate-Bottled These words indicate that the wine was produced and bottled on the property where the grapes were grown.

Extra Dry A contradictory term used on Champagne labels meaning somewhat sweet. The degree of sweetness varies.

Fiasco The Italian name for flask—the straw-covered, round-bottomed container popularly associated with Chianti.

Fine Champagne Not a sparkling wine but a brandy from the areas of Grande Champagne and Petite Champagne, near the town of Cognac.

Fining A traditional process of clarification by the addition of certain substances to the wine in the barrel. The fining medium settles to the bottom carrying with it the fine suspended particles.

Flor The variety of yeast giving the character peculiar to dry sherries. It occurs naturally in Spain; in other countries the fermented wine is inoculated with it.

Flowery A term denoting the fragrance of blossoms in a wine's bouquet or aroma.

Fortified Wine Wine to which alcohol has been added, usually in the form of brandy, such as Sherry, Port, and Muscatel.

Foxiness The controversial pronounced aroma characteristic of many native American grapes. Some like it, some don't.

Frappé The notation *Servir frappé* is sometimes found on French white wine labeling; it means—Serve iced or chilled.

Fruity Term applied to a fine young wine which has the aroma and flavor of fresh fruit.

Full Pleasingly strong in flavor, bouquet, or taste.

Generic Appellation of wine type having certain characteristics not related to its actual origin. U.S. wines labeled Chablis, Port, Rhine Wine are using the generic appellation. See *Varietal.*

Grand Vin French for "Great Wine." Where it appears unsupported by a truly great name, it is usually as meaningless as *Vin Fin.*

Green Term applied to wine of excessive acidity.

Hard Winetaster's term for a wine with excessive tannin. Not necessarily a fault in a young wine, where it may indicate a long maturity.

Haut French word meaning high, sometimes upper, or top, all in a geographic sense, and not as an implication of superior quality. Applied to Sauterne in the U.S. it indicates sweetness.

Heavy Excessive alcohol content without a corresponding balance of flavor.

Kellerabfüllung Notation on German wine labels meaning "cellar bottling," the equivalent of the French *mis en bouteilles au Château,* or estate-bottled. Sometimes *Kellerabzug* is used for the same purpose.

Labrusca The prinicipal species of the native American grape, *Vitis labrusca,* typical examples of which are the Concord, Catawba, and Ives.

Lees The sediment deposited in cooperage before bottling. The lees are left behind by racking.

Light A complimentary term applied to pleasant refreshing wines; the opposite of full-bodied.

Must The grape juice before it is fermented.

Musty Unpleasant "mousy" odor and flavor, similar to moldy, usually due to unclean cellar.

Nature French term equivalent to *Brut* or *Naturwein* in German, meaning no sweetener has been added.

Nose Professional winetaster term describing quality of *bouquet.*

Original Abfüllung This precise notation on a German label indicates that the wine was grown, made, and bottled at the vineyard by the owners.

Oxidation The chemical process of absorption of oxygen from the air, and the corresponding changes for good or bad.

Pourriture Noble French for "noble rot," or *Edelfaule.*

Press A machine which, by applying direct pressure, forces the juice from the grapes. There are many types of presses, ranging from the ancient hand-operated wooden press to sophisticated hydraulic machines made of stainless steel.

Racking The process whereby clear wine is drawn off its lees and sediment, and transferred from one storage container to another.

Riddling In Champagne-making, the process of working the sediment into the neck of the bottle during the second fermentation. Traditionally a hand operation, it is now being done mechanically in many wineries, particularly in the United States.

Rotundifolia A secondary species of native American grapes having a muscadine flavor. A typical example of *Vitis rotundifolia* is the Scuppernung of the Carolinas.

Sec French word for dry. *Secco,* in Italian, is used similarly.

Sediment The solid matter thrown by wine during fermentation and aging. It is more pronounced and abundant in red wines than in whites. In the aging process it sometimes forms a crust on the wall of the bottle. Wines with heavy sedimentation must be decanted before serving.

Sekt Generic type name of German sparkling wines.

Soft Term describing the pleasant smoothness of wines of low astringency. Not related to sweetness.

Sour A disagreeable taste sensation, acid and vinegary, indicating a spoiled, undrinkable wine. Not to be confused with tartness, astringency, or dryness.

Spätlese On a German wine label this word indicates a natural (unsweetened) wine, made from riper grapes picked after the normal vintage. The wine is usually fuller-bodied, and a bit sweeter than the other wines of the same vineyard made with the grapes picked earlier. Literally means "late picking."

Still Wine A non-effervescent wine in which the carbon dioxide gas, formed during fermentation, has all escaped. The opposite of sparkling wine.

Tart The sharp, astringent taste of fruit acid, like the taste of a McIntosh apple. When present in a moderate degree, tartness lends a pleasant freshness to a wine.

Tawny The brownish-red color acquired by some red wines in aging. The characteristic color of Tawny Port.

Varietal The wine name taken from the grape variety used to make it. The following are some of the varietal names: Pinot Noir, Delaware, Cabernet Sauvignon, Pinot Chardonnay, Riesling, etc. See *Generic*.

Vigneron In France this name usually means a skilled vineyard worker, but the term has been extended to include vineyardists, wine growers and wine makers.

Vin de Carafe French term for good, plain wine, usually sold in bulk to restaurants and served in a *carafe*, or plain decanter. The equivalent in the U.S. of the inexpensive jug wines.

Vin Fin This much abused French term, with its implication of quality, is too often used indiscriminately to have much weight unless backed by more significant data on the label.

Vinifera The most important of the 32 species of vines making up the genus *Vitis* in the botanical classification. In the genus, some 20 are native to America, and 11 native to Asia. *Vitis vinifera*, with the exception of some hybrids, is the specie of grape from which all the wines of Europe, Africa, South America, and California are made. It is being successfully introduced in other wine regions such as New York State.

Vinification This broad term covers the whole process of turning grapes into wine, except for the vineyard operations. It includes fermentation, clarification, and aging.

Vin Ordinaire What the French, without derogation, call their everyday, simple, ordinary wines. They are usually sold unlabeled, either in bulk or in bottles.

Vintage The harvesting, crushing, and fermentation of grapes into wine. This term is also applied to the crop of grapes or the wine of one season.

Vintage Wine A wine labeled with the year in which all the grapes from which it was made were harvested and made into wine. When supported by other information, it usually implies a better quality than its non-vintage counterpart.

Vintner This broad term, once applied only to wholesale wine merchants, now includes wine growers, wine makers, wine blenders, etc.

Viticulture The cultivation of the vine, also the science of grape production.

Woody Term describing the characteristic odor of wine aged in wooden cooperage for an extended period. The odor is like that of wet wood.

SUGGESTED READING

Here is a list of books to provide the reader with further guidance in wine enjoyment. All are full of interesting wine lore. Those marked with an asterisk (*) are available in paperback editions.

Adams, Leon D., **The Commonsense Book of Wine***, *David McKay Co., Inc., New York, N.Y., 1960*

Amerine, M.A. and Singleton, V.L., **Wine, An Introduction for Americans***, *Univ. of Calif. Press, Berkeley, Calif., 1965*

Bespaloff, Alexis, **The Signet Book of Wine***, *New American Library, Inc., New York, N.Y., 1971*

Churchill, Creighton, **The World of Wines***, *Macmillan Co., New York, N.Y., 1967*

Dorozynski, Alexander, and Bell, Bibiane, **The Wine Book,** *Western Publishing Co., New York, N.Y., 1969*

Grossman, Harold J , **Grossman's Guide to Wine, Spirits, and Beers,** rev. ed., *Charles Scribner's Sons, New York, N.Y., 1964*

Hannum, Hurst, and Blumberg, Robert S., **The Fine Wines of California***, *Doubleday & Co., Inc., New York, N.Y., 1971*

Johnson, Hugh, **The World Atlas of Wine,** *Simon & Schuster, Inc., New York, N.Y., 1971*

Johnson, Hugh, **Wine,** *Simon & Schuster, Inc., New York, N.Y., 1967*

Lichine, Alexis, **Alexis Lichine's Encyclopedia of Wines and Spirits,** id , **Wines of France**, rev. 5th ed., *Alfred A. Knopf, New York, N.Y., 1967 Alfred A. Knopf, New York, N.Y., 1969*

Lucia, Salvatore Pablo, M. D., **Wine and Your Well Being*,** *Wine Advisory Board, San Francisco, Calif., 1971*

Massee, William E., **Massee's Wine Handbook,** rev. ed., *Doubleday & Co., Inc., New York, N.Y., 1971*

Melville, John, **Guide to California Wines***, rev. by Jefferson Morgan, 3rd ed., *Nourse Publishing Co., San Carlos, Calif., 1968*

Rowe, Percy, **The Wines of Canada**, *McGraw-Hill Book Co., New York, N.Y.*

Schoonmaker, Frank, **Encyclopedia of Wine,** 4th rev. ed., *Hastings House Publishers, Inc., New York, N.Y., 1969*

Simon, André L., **Everybody's Guide to Wines and Spirits**, *Transatlantic Art Inc., Levittown, N.Y.*

Simon, André L., **Wines of the World,** *McGraw-Hill Book Co., New York, N.Y., 1967*

Storm, John, **An Invitation to Wines***, *Simon & Schuster Inc., New York, N.Y., 1963*

Taylor, Greyton H., and Vine, Richard P., **Treasury of Wine and Wine Cookery,** *Harper & Row, New York, N.Y., 1963*

Waugh, Alec, **Wines and Spirits**, *Time-Life Books, New York, 1968.*

ACKNOWLEDGMENTS

This little book, simple and limited as it is, could not have been written without the help and encouragement of hundreds of kind and generous people in and around the wine industry, both here and abroad. Individuals, wine companies, wine institutes and societies have shared information, provided photographs and labels, and made me welcome on extensive tours of their facilities.

I am particularly grateful to C. "Tony" Kahmann whose expert guidance, kindly patience, and tireless efforts made me fully aware of the accomplishments and potential of California's wineries.

The California Wine Institute was the major contributor of superb photographs, and an inexhaustible source of help in many ways.

The wine institutes and associations of Alsace, Argentina, Australia, Bordeaux, Canada, Chile, Portugal, Spain, and many other wine producing regions were most cooperative in making valuable material available.

The wine companies, such as Boordy Vineyards, Browne Vintners, The Christian Brothers, Pleasant Valley Wine Co., Schramsberg Vineyards, Taylor Wine Co., and Wente Brothers deserve special thanks for their help and encouragement.

I am also grateful for the help and advice of countless individuals whose help and advice has been invaluable: Joe Concannon, William Dieppe, Dr. Konstantin Frank, Robert M. Ivie, Louis Latour, Jim Lucas, George McRory, Otto Meyer, Baron Ricasoli, Dr. V. L. Singleton, Walter Taylor, Brother Timothy, and Richard P. Vine, to single out but a few.

PHOTO CREDITS

Australian News & Information Bureau: pp. 21M, 92, 149; California Wine Institute: pp. 8, 9, 10T, 10B, 11T, 11B, 13, 17, 19T, 20, 22, 23, 24, 25B, 37, 124, 125, 126 through 141; Casa de Portugal: p. 88; Comité Interprofessionnel du Vin d'Alsace: p. 10M; Conseil Interprofessionnel du Vin de Bordeaux; pp. 56, 57; The Christian Brothers; pp. 33, 35, 144, 145; Henri Fluchère: pp. 71, 107, 108, 110, 117, 119, 120, 121; Instituto Nacional de Vitivinicultura: p. 101; Elmer S. Phillips: p. 49; Pleasant Valley Wine Co.: pp. 11M, 21T; The Sherry Institute of Spain: p. 2; Sleepy Hollow Restorations, Inc.: p. 29; Suntory: p. 105; Taylor Wine Co.: pp. 18, 19M, 19B, 21B, 25T, 47; Greyton H. Taylor Wine Museum; pp. 142, 143; Walter S. Taylor: p. 27.

INDEX

B C D E